HIGH HOPES

HIGH HOPES

Ursula Dubosarsky

VIKING

Penguin Books Australia Ltd
487 Maroondah Highway, PO Box 257
Ringwood, Victoria, 3134, Australia
Penguin Books Ltd
Harmondsworth, Middlesex, England
Viking Penguin, A Division of Penguin Books USA Inc.
375 Hudson Street, New York, New York 10014, USA
Penguin Books Canada Limited
2801 John Street, Markham, Ontario, Canada, L3R 1B4
Penguin Books (N.Z.) Ltd
182–190 Wairau Road, Auckland 10, New Zealand

First published by Penguin Books Australia, 1990
This Viking edition published 1990
1 3 5 7 9 10 8 6 4 2
Copyright © Ursula Dubosarsky, 1990

Typeset in Malaysia by Seng Teik
Made and printed in Australia by Australian Print Group

National Library of Australia
Cataloguing-in-Publication data:

Dubosarsky, Ursula, 1961– .
High hopes.

ISBN 0 670 835609.
I. Title.
A823.3

The publisher gratefully acknowledges permission to reproduce copyright
material in the form of extracts taken from the following:

Fishback, Margaret: 'Sofia', from *Making Music Your Own*, published by Silver
Burdett Company. Reprinted by permission of General Learning Corporation.
(Pages 105–6)

'Poison' in *Encyclopaedia Britannica*, 14th edition (1973), 18:99. (Page 65)

To darling Avi

Julia lived with her father and grandmother above a delicatessen in Oxford Street. During the day Julia's father worked in the delicatessen and at night he came upstairs, ate dinner and went to sleep. His name was George and he was from Argentina. Of course, his name wasn't really George but Jorge. You pronounce it 'Horhay' in Spanish, which is what they speak in Argentina. But in Australia he was called George.

Julia's mother died in a hospital, just around the corner from the delicatessen, when Julia was born. Not many people died even in those days from having a baby, but Julia's mother did. Poor George was very sad. Julia's mother's name was Isabel – she was from Chile and Julia thought she was very beautiful. George had lots of photographs of her. She had black hair and fat cheeks, but her body was thin, so thin she almost didn't look grown up.

By the time Julia was nine years old, she started helping George and his assistant, Emily, in the shop. Emily had grey hair and glasses and was very polite – with the customers, anyway. She also had four children and lots of grandchildren and nephews and nieces who left messages for her on the telephone.

Julia's grandmother didn't help serve the customers, but sat upright behind the counter in a high-backed chair to keep an eye on things. Back in Argentina, when George's father was alive, they'd kept a hardware store, and she liked to compare the businesses and give George advice. She would have liked to give Emily advice as well, except Emily didn't speak any Spanish and Julia's grandmother didn't speak any English. This was probably just as well, as Julia's grandmother could be quite rude and Emily mightn't have appreciated it.

Julia loved the shop. She loved the things George sold – the six different kinds of olives, the five kinds of pâté, the squid in jars, the halva from Israel, the green tea from Brazil, the quince jam sold in solid blocks like cheese. She loved the smell of the almond twists, the machine that cut salami and the fetta floating in curdy water like icebergs. Of course, some of the things that George sold were not so nice, especially the cows' feet and the pickled tongue, but Julia tried not to notice them.

There was a long line of shops along both sides of the street where George's delicatessen was – a bakery, a café, three or four restaurants, a newsagent, a gift shop, a hardware shop, a second-hand furniture shop and at least two fruit and vegetable shops. There was also another delicatessen, which George called the 'opposition' and sometimes he sent Julia down as a spy to see how many customers they were getting and what they were charging for peppercorn liverwurst.

Quite a few Jewish people came in to George's shop. George was Jewish, and when it was the time of the Jewish New Year, he put signs in the window saying

SHANA TOVA, which means 'Happy New Year'. He thought it might attract customers, which it did, judging by the number of people who came in and wished him 'Shana Tova' in return. George sold special breads and biscuits and poppy-seed cakes and other things that Jewish people have to eat at religious festivals. George never bothered about the festivals himself. In fact, he'd only been to a synagogue once the whole time he'd been in Australia. That was when Isabel died, which was perhaps why he'd never been again.

By the time Julia was twelve years old and in sixth class at school, she felt quite adult and worldly-wise. It seemed to her that George and her grandmother were innocents in a wild world, who needed her careful protection. Perhaps it was because they depended on her so much to speak English. At home, in the rooms above the delicatessen, they almost always spoke Spanish. Julia's grandmother didn't speak English at all, and although George spoke quite a lot of English, Julia felt it was rather peculiar and often hard to understand. She had to translate the special instructions that came through the mail from the government, and help him fill in forms. She also had to explain jokes on the television, although she didn't like to much, as by the time she'd managed to explain one joke to both George and her grandmother's satisfaction, she'd missed the next three.

Not that George worried about his English – he thought he spoke perfectly well. When Julia suggested that perhaps he should go and do a course at tech., he never seemed very interested. Julia couldn't understand his reluctance – after all, Isabel had done a course at tech. – not in English, admittedly, but leatherwork. George was always showing people the certificate she'd got

3

for it, when he was in a sentimental mood and remembering how artistic she was.

Of course, Julia was the sort of person who worried about lots and lots of things – particularly to do with George. She worried about what George ate and what George drank and what time he went to bed and what time he got up and how hard he worked and how much money he was making and the kinds of friends he had. But at the time of this story, George's English was what worried her the most.

After all, she mightn't always be there to translate for him. She might drop dead one day like her mother. She might get run over, or kidnapped, or sold to a white slave trader and then what would George do? He might be forced to sell all their worldly possessions to pay off a luxury lounge suite he didn't know he was signing for – she'd read about this sort of thing in books. Or worse still, an important announcement might come on the television ordering all residents of Oxford Street to evacuate immediately, and George and her grandmother would just sit there happily watching 'Rosa de Lejos' while a terrible poisonous gas came under the door and they would go blue all over and choke to death.

Julia became especially preoccupied with these sorts of thoughts after coming home from school one day to find George in the middle of an argument with a man in a khaki-green suit. At least, the man in the suit was arguing – George was looking mystified. Alarmed, Julia thrust her satchel behind the fridge and hurried over to them.

'What's going on?' she whispered to Emily, who was standing to one side, watching.

'I'm not quite sure, dear. I only came in halfway,' said

Emily. 'But they seem to be having some kind of personal disagreement.'

'It's not funny!' shouted the man, banging his hand on the counter.

'No!' agreed George at once, adopting a frown.

'I specifically mentioned,' continued the man more quietly, taking a handkerchief out of his breast pocket and carefully wiping away the fingerprints he'd left on the silver counter top, 'that my wife and I cannot abide hot food.'

'I remember!' said George cooperatively. 'And I thought – strange man.'

'Then why,' said the man, raising his voice again, 'did you sell me over half a kilo of salami almost entirely composed of chilli!'

'You don't like chilli?' said George, surprised. 'Why didn't you say so?'

The man in the khaki suit breathed deeply, and looked as if he were about to say something that most people would rather not hear, but he didn't. He breathed heavily again, stuffed his handkerchief in his top pocket and marched out.

'What happened?' Julia demanded, facing George squarely so that he couldn't avoid her.

George rolled his eyes and gave her a mischievous smile. 'Nothing, my love,' he said. 'Just a poor crazy man.'

'But what was he complaining about?' Julia persisted. 'People don't just start shouting for nothing.'

'He came here yesterday,' said George, sounding injured, 'asking for salami but nothing hot. So what? Who sells hot salami? You keep it in the fridge. So I sold him the most delicious, and now he comes back and complains about the chilli.'

'Don't worry about it, Julia,' said Emily briskly, stepping forward as another customer came in. 'That fellow just likes to make a fuss.'

'But you know what people mean when they say "hot",' said Julia to George sternly. 'You know they mean "*picante*" and not "*caliente*".'

'I know, I know, but I forgot,' said George, grimacing. 'Sometimes I forget things. It's okay. Anyway, what's salami without a bit of chilli? Come on!'

Julia was very disturbed by this incident, and completely dissatisfied with George's explanation of it. Who knew how many customers walked in with perfectly reasonable requests, only to be dismissed by George as poor crazy people? They could lose dozens of customers a week that way! And next time it might be more serious. Someone might come in and ask for a glass of water to take their heart pills with and George would laugh and give them vodka and before you knew it they would drop down dead. Then George would get taken to court and sued and deported back to Argentina, and then they might put him in the army, or prison and he would get eaten by rats.

Julia was thinking grimly about this the following Sunday morning when she and George were walking down Oxford Street to buy the Sunday paper – George liked reading the classified advertisements. The delicatessen was closed on Sundays and so were a lot of the other shops, but the newsagent was always open. It was one of Julia's favourite shops – at least twice the size of the delicatessen and filled with shelves and shelves of interesting things. There were books and cards and magazines and toys, staplers in several sizes and colours so that they looked like a family of mother and father staplers with children ranging from teenagers to babies. There were different coloured envelopes, and packets of things for parties and enormous bags of chips and honeycomb. There was always something to look at if George met someone he knew, as he usually did, and stood around talking for twenty minutes.

That particular morning, George met the old man who supplied him with four of the six kinds of olives that he sold. He was an unusual-looking person, with a long fluffy grey beard, and most of the time he wore a furry black hat – the kind of thing the Queen might wear on a chilly day. He was from Russia and had very blue eyes. At least, he was sort of from Russia – really he was from Czechoslovakia, or perhaps it was East Germany which used to be Austria. It was a very complicated story, anyway, and neither George nor Julia had ever really understood it, although he had explained it to them both several times.

The old man was in the newsagent buying the German newspaper. German was his native language – Julia had heard him speaking it on the street with his children who were tall, elegant blond adults with very clean hair. George, who was in a good mood that morning, slapped him on the back and started talking about the soccer. Julia looked at some packets of drawing pins, some wedding invitations and a special thank-you card to send to your doctor. The old man with the beard was smiling at George politely as if he didn't quite follow.

Julia stepped out onto the footpath, which was shiny and black and wet from early morning rain. She stood on her tiptoes and spun around on one foot. As she did so, she was attracted by a sign in the newsagency window.

There were always notices in this window, usually advertising lost cats or nursing home fêtes. Sometimes there were handwritten signs saying that a student was willing to do anything, or a Portuguese lady would iron with honesty. Once Julia herself had even put up a notice when her grandmother lost her reading glasses on the street. She had taken a lot of trouble over the wording of the sign, and had enthusiastically written at the end: REWARD FOR FINDER, without knowing what this reward might be. Luckily no one ever rang up to claim the reward, which was not surprising, as her grandmother had not lost her glasses on the street at all, but had accidentally let them slip behind the sofa where George discovered them three days later when he was doing the vacuuming.

The sign that caught Julia's eye that morning was new and clean, placed on top of a yellowed notice about a primary school centenary ball. It was neatly printed in capitals in green texta, and had little holly leaves decorating the edges, although it was nowhere near Christmas. The sign said:

ENGLISH TAUGHT IN YOUR OWN HOME BY QUALIFIED TEACHER. NO CHARGE. VOLUNTEER COUNCIL-SPONSORED PROGRAM.

Then it had a telephone number, followed in smaller letters by:

ASK FOR ANABEL.

Then in big letters again, rather mysteriously:

YOUR TROUBLES WILL SOON BE OVER.

'ENGLISH TAUGHT IN YOUR OWN HOME.' Naturally Julia's first thoughts were of George. Now she knew she could never get him to go to school to learn, but 'IN YOUR OWN HOME' – surely that would be different. It couldn't hurt to try, could it, particularly if it were free. Julia read the sign again. Funny to spell 'Anabel' with only one 'n' – unless it was a mistake, which wasn't such a good recommendation for a teacher. But still . . .

Julia poked her head back inside the newsagency. George was in the middle of telling the Russian a joke in a loud exuberant voice. Julia sighed. It was hard enough when George tried to tell a joke in English, let alone to someone who didn't understand English very well in the first place. In Spanish, George could tell long and complicated jokes with lots of funny voices and people who understood Spanish laughed quite a lot. But now the Russian was merely looking bewildered, and saying 'Yes' at intervals.

Julia walked over and took the pen he always kept for emergencies out of George's left pocket. George smiled at her and continued telling his joke. Julia slipped back outside and wrote down Anabel's phone number on the back of an old government bus pass that she'd bought from a church fête for five cents. It had belonged to someone called Grant Event, which was why she had bought it. Grant Event – if you said it quickly it sounded like something at the Easter Show – or was that Grand Parade? Anyway, she wrote Anabel's number down in the space above the government regulations, then went back inside to George.

The Russian had escaped, and George was standing at the counter waiting to pay for his paper.

'What have you been up to, my queen?' he said to her in Spanish, pinching the skin at the back of her neck.

'Oh nothing,' Julia replied in English.

She slid Grant Event's bus pass back into her pocket surreptitiously and gave George his pen. It would be better, perhaps, not to mention her idea about Anabel just yet. She would ring and speak to Anabel herself first. George was sure to take it all the wrong way. He was so excitable.

2

Almost a week passed before Julia rang the number and asked for Anabel. It wasn't that she forgot: she remembered so often that she knew the number off by heart. She rehearsed what she would say to Anabel as she sat in her natural science class at school, her creative expression class and especially her social studies class, when they had to watch a television program about elections in the Philippines.

But still she came back home to the delicatessen each day after school and didn't telephone. She would put her satchel behind the refrigerator, eat a shortbread biscuit and talk to Emily about her grandson's new hang-glider. She watched 'Rosa de Lejos' with George and her grandmother and ate sweet corn and potato chips on toast. She played chess with George and Patience with herself. Every night for a week she went to bed and wished she'd already rung, because now she would have to spend the whole of the next day worrying about when she would.

It wasn't until Saturday night that she finally called. She'd spent the day playing with the new puppy that belonged to the boy whose father owned the fruit and vegetable shop two doors down. The puppy was black and white with a long fluffy tail like an ostrich feather and it had tiny sweet teeth that tickled when it nibbled her hand.

Julia and the boy played with the puppy in the lane behind the shops where there were less cars. The boy didn't live above a shop like she did – he lived in a house with a big garden and two other dogs. On weekends he came to help his father out at work, although Julia had never seen him do anything much and noticed that his father seemed to get on perfectly well without him during the week.

The whole time Julia played with the puppy, she was thinking about Anabel and George and how she must ring that night or else. She decided to pretend that she was in the war and had to get a vital message through on the phone to headquarters. She became so involved with this idea, and the story she invented in her head got so complicated and dangerous, that she practically forgot altogether the real reason for the phone call. But when the boy picked up his puppy, climbed into his father's truck and went home, she remembered and returned to the delicatessen with a very determined frown.

George was working in the shop alone because Emily had to leave early to visit her grandson in hospital after his hang-gliding accident. Emily's grandchildren and nephews and nieces were always having accidents. Emily said that they were born unlucky – although when you considered how many accidents they managed to have without being killed, you might just as well say that they were born lucky instead.

'Taste this, *amorcito*,' George said to Julia as she walked in. ('Amorcito' means 'little love' in Spanish.) He waved a knife with a smear of something on it at her.

'Macedonian halva.'

Julia took the substance onto her finger and sucked it off cautiously. Halva always made her feel ill. She didn't really like sweet food all that much, something George found difficult to understand. Julia was skinny, like her mother, whereas George was thick with large round muscles on his arms and legs.

'Delicious,' said Julia, not very convincingly to the customer whom George was tempting and who had just tasted some himself. 'Macedonian,' she added, unable to think of anything else.

Tempting customers was one of George's favourite occupations. He would offer a taste of this and a taste of that, discuss recipe variations and ways of serving things. George respected customers who took a long time to make a decision, because that was the way he bought things himself. It was lucky he had Emily working for him, as she served the customers very swiftly and politely and did not encourage conversation. Julia often thought that if it weren't for Emily, there would be queues stretching miles out the door and they would never make any money at all.

Julia abandoned George, the customer and the Macedonian halva and ran up the stairs two at a time. Her grandmother was watching the Rugby League on television – 'Rosa De Lejos' wasn't on during weekends. Julia kissed her grandmother on the lips and sat down in the chair next to the telephone. Her heart seemed to be beating very loudly. She took Grant Event's bus pass from her jeans' pocket and dialled the number.

After three rings, a woman's voice answered. Julia breathed deeply. 'Can I speak to Anabel, please?'

'This is Anabel,' said the voice.

'Oh,' said Julia. She had secretly hoped that Anabel

would be out playing hockey or ice skating or any of the other things the name Anabel suggested.

'It's about the English lessons in your own home,' Julia said.

'Oh yes.' The voice was encouraging. 'What would you like to know?'

'Well, will you come?' Julia asked bluntly. 'To my home?'

'Um,' replied the voice. 'You don't need English lessons, do you?'

'My father does,' explained Julia. 'But you have to be careful, you know.'

'Oh yes?'

'Yes,' Julia replied firmly, trying to think of a word she had written in her vocabulary book two weeks ago. Subtle. That was it.

'You have to be subtle. He's a bit thingy, you see. About having lessons,' said Julia, adding desperately, 'You know.'

'I think I understand,' said the voice of Anabel, not sounding very confident. 'You can trust me. Where do you live?'

Julia told her.

'And what time should I come?'

'Oh well.' Julia thought for a moment, looking about the room. Her grandmother had dropped off to sleep, clutching the television's remote control box to her stomach. It would be easier if Anabel came when Julia was at school. Then she wouldn't have to explain anything until it was over.

'In the daytime would be best. Maybe on Monday.'

'Well,' said the voice, sounding busy. 'What about Monday at two?'

'Great.' Julia was relieved.

'What's his name? Your father, I mean.'

Julia told her.

'And yours?'

'Julia,' said Julia suspiciously. 'But you mustn't tell him I rang you. He mustn't know I had anything to do with it.'

'No, no, no. Don't worry. I understand. What country are you from?'

'My father is from Argentina,' replied Julia, 'but I was born in Bourke Street. In a hospital,' she added, in case that sounded peculiar.

'Right,' said the voice. 'And what's your father's English like?'

'Terrible,' said Julia, without hesitation, thinking that Anabel might like a challenge.

'Okay then.' Anabel's voice sounded a little disturbed. 'Well, I'll do my best. I'll be in on Monday then. He won't be working or anything at that time, will he?'

'Oh no,' Julia lied.

'Okay.' Anabel's voice sounded like a piece of paper being folded up. 'Monday it is then. No names, no pack drills. Thanks for ringing.'

'Bye.'

Julia put down the phone, excited, but puzzled. No names, no pack drills? What an odd person. She stood up, rubbing her face with her hands. She could still smell the fur of the puppy all over them.

Of course, she couldn't tell George that Anabel was coming. George was sure to be cross and make her ring back and cancel everything. It would be so much better to surprise him. Especially seeing Anabel had promised to be subtle.

3

Monday at Julia's school was sports day. She had to wear a special uniform with a white stripe down one side and she was supposed to wear ribbons in her hair the colour of her house, which was red. She didn't mind the uniform, and she didn't even mind the ribbons, but she hated sport.

She hated people shouting at her and telling her to get the ball and groaning when she invariably didn't. She wouldn't have minded swimming, which they did in summer in the Domain, if they'd just let her swim up and down pretending she was a dolphin, but they wouldn't, of course. They insisted on having races – worst of all, team races, which was just as bad as netball or soccer.

That Monday afternoon, the afternoon of George's first English lesson, it was softball. Of all team sports, softball was perhaps the least terrible. Julia could stand in the outfield so far out that the others would forget she was still part of the game, and she could entertain herself by singing or watching the insects in the grass. When her team's turn came round to bat, she (and everyone else) made sure that she was the last to go on, which usually meant not at all.

They played softball out at a field called Moore Park and Julia would get the bus home. That Monday, it had been a dismal game in which everyone, including the teacher, had shouted at her for not even noticing that the ball had miraculously reached her until the other team had got three players to home base.

Julia got off the bus a stop earlier than usual. She wanted to be absolutely sure that Anabel would be gone by the time she got home. The curious part of her naturally wanted to meet Anabel and see what she was like, but the nervous part of her proved stronger.

She dawdled to the delicatessen, counting cats along the way. It was surprising how many there were when you looked for them. But it didn't stop that slightly sick feeling in her stomach. What if Anabel were a disaster? What if George were terribly angry with her? But George was never angry, just depressed, which was worse. What if George were depressed? Julia almost moaned. She would have turned pale as well, if it had been possible for her to be any paler than she already was.

When she finally reached the front door of the shop, she walked in with her head bent down, pretending to be concentrating on a twist in her satchel strap. But George wasn't there. Her grandmother was sitting on her high stool behind the counter watching the ice hockey, with the sound turned down, on a little black-and-white television that George had suspended on the wall to entertain the customers when they had to wait a long time.

Emily was making a cheese and gherkin wholegrain sandwich for a tall woman in a black and gold dress.

'Salt and pepper?' said Emily.

'Neither, thank you,' replied the tall woman. 'But could I have a little grated carrot?'

Julia slid behind the counter and kissed her grandmother.

'Where's Dad?' she asked Emily, picking up a yellow pickle with some tongs and popping it in her mouth.

'Upstairs, dear,' said Emily, wrapping up the sandwich in grease-proof paper and putting it in a white paper bag.

The pickle was unbearably hot. Julia felt her face going pink and all the roots of her hair tingled in pain. She spat the pickle out into her hand and rushed over to the double sink, turning on the cold water tap into her mouth. It occurred to her that it mustn't look very hygienic to the woman in the black and gold dress.

'Upstairs?' she gasped between gulps of water. 'Daddy's upstairs?' she said to her grandmother in Spanish.

'With a woman,' replied her grandmother, keeping her eye on the ice hockey and tying the ribbon on the end of Julia's plait into a bow.

'He's with a lady,' said Emily, who didn't speak Spanish and wasn't about to learn. 'From the council or some such place. Teaching him English.' Emily looked amused. 'They've been at it two hours at least.'

'Oh.'

Julia supposed that must be a good sign. Surely George would have sent Anabel away long ago if he'd been angry about it.

'Do you need any help?' she asked Emily hopefully, who having got rid of the cheese and gherkin sandwich was now at work on a tabouli and ricotta roll.

'Oh no, don't you worry dear. It's been very quiet this afternoon,' said Emily, adding, not very cheerfully, 'Quiet as the grave.'

Julia climbed the stairs slowly and softly. She could hear voices coming from the living room. One was George's, of course, and the other she recognised as Anabel's. Reaching the top step, she turned the corner quickly and walked inside.

George and a girl were sitting at the collapsible card-table with a thick new note-pad in front of them. George was painstakingly writing something down, while the girl who must be Anabel was making an encouraging noise. She had very straight short brown hair, held back from her face with what looked like about a hundred bobby pins. She was wearing pink glasses which were half-falling of her nose, and she had freckles and a black mole on her cheek.

'Hello,' said Julia.

Anabel looked up and smiled. George smiled too, but he seemed embarrassed, and he stood up, nearly knocking the card-table over.

'Julia, my love,' said George. 'This is Miss Anabel. She is an English teacher.'

George made this announcement very carefully and clearly, quite unlike his usual rough-and-tumble English.

'How do you do?' said Julia. 'Is Daddy a good student?'

'Oh, I think we're making progress,' said Anabel, not sounding nearly as business-like as she had on the phone. She giggled and pushed her glasses back up the bridge of her nose. Julia noticed that the right arm of the glasses had broken off the main frame and was tied back on with a piece of hat elastic.

'Actually,' said Anabel, 'I think we've probably made enough progress for one day. What do you think, Mr . . . er . . . George?'

'Yes! Yes! Enough!' agreed George with a dramatic

clap of his hands. 'Now we must have some tea!'

George had an idea that Australian women like tea, although most of the ones Julia knew, mainly the mothers of her school friends, drank coffee or Diet Coca-Cola.

'Oh . . . thank you . . . you mustn't bother . . .' said Anabel, standing up from the card-table.

'Do you like vanilla biscuits?' asked Julia. 'Because my grandmother made some yesterday.'

'Oh,' said Anabel again. 'How nice . . . thank you.'

George, beaming broadly, disappeared into the kitchen and began clanking around with the kettle and teacups. Julia and Anabel stood looking at each other. Julia opened her mouth. Anabel giggled. Julia closed her mouth. Anabel whispered:

'I hope I was subtle enough. I didn't mention you at all.'

'Are you really from the council?' Julia asked.

'Well, in a way,' said Anabel. 'The volunteer teaching program's sponsored by the council. Or at least not exactly sponsored. But it was through the council I got involved, you see.'

'Oh.' What a vague person.

'His English isn't all that bad, you know,' continued Anabel in a low voice. 'You had me frightened – I thought he wouldn't even be able to say his name.'

'Oh.'

George called out from the kitchen in Spanish, telling Julia to go downstairs and get her grandmother to come up and have some tea.

'But she's watching TV,' Julia objected, also in Spanish.

'I'm sure she'd rather have tea with Miss Anabel than watch TV,' insisted George.

'I'm just going to get my grandmother,' Julia explained to Anabel, who was looking mystified. 'Daddy wants her to meet you.'

'Oh, please!' said Anabel, alarmed. 'Please don't disturb her!'

Julia would have been quite happy to oblige Anabel, but at that moment she heard her grandmother's footsteps on the stairs. She ran out onto the landing. Her grandmother, reaching the top step, gave her a look which meant 'Well? So?' and then waddled into the living room. She smiled at Anabel and sat herself down on the sofa. Anabel sat nervously next to her, pushing a bobby pin back into her hair.

George called out from the kitchen: 'Tea, Mama?'

Julia's grandmother then pulled herself back up from the sofa, went out to the kitchen and returned with a square red tartan tin in her hand. With a slight struggle, she opened it up. Inside were layers of brown biscuits with fork marks on the top. She offered the tin to Anabel. '*Come mucho*,' she said, nodding vigorously.

'That means "Eat a lot",' Julia said. 'She probably thinks you're too skinny.'

Looking surprised, as she was not actually very skinny at all, Anabel took a biscuit and shoved it into her mouth.

'*Hablas Idishe?*' asked Julia's grandmother, watching her eat with a hopeful expression on her face.

'She wants to know if you can speak Yiddish,' said Julia.

'Well, no, actually,' confessed Anabel apologetically, her mouth full of biscuit. 'Only English.'

Julia translated. Her grandmother sighed and sat down on the sofa again. George came out of the kitchen with a glass of lime cordial which he handed to Julia, knowing she didn't drink tea. As usual, he had made it far too sweet. George had such a sweet tooth, he even sprinkled sugar on his ice-cream. Julia followed him back into the kitchen, tipped half the cordial into the sink and refilled the glass with water. George, busy organising the teacups, had left the empty kettle on the stove. Julia turned off the gas and examined the base of the kettle. It wasn't too badly burnt, this time.

George balanced the teacups along one arm like a waiter in the movies and somehow held the teapot and a carton of milk in his other hand. He laid everything on the coffee table, pushing yesterday's paper from the table onto the floor. He smiled at Anabel and she shovelled another vanilla biscuit in her mouth.

George poured the tea. He asked Anabel where she lived and she said Newtown, not far, really. He asked her if she had a car and what type it was and what engine it was and what colour it was and where did she buy it and how old was it? Julia's ears switched off as they usually did when George started talking about cars. Poor Anabel, she thought.

She sat on the floor with her glass of lime cordial and leaned back against the coffee table. She felt rather pleased with herself. It looked as though her idea had been a real success. She gulped the pale green drink and closed her eyes, relaxed. Anabel would have George reading, writing and speaking English in no time at all.

4

Over the next few weeks Anabel became a regular figure at the delicatessen, coming for lessons every two or three days. At first she came during the day, when the shop was open, but Emily complained. Emily was polite, even when she was complaining, but she was also very firm. She wasn't being paid to manage the shop, she said, and she didn't want the responsibility if a disaster happened while George was upstairs with his books.

Actually, Julia thought the chances of a disaster happening were much greater when George was downstairs in the shop than when he was upstairs with his books. Emily was so efficient it was impossible to imagine any sort of disaster happening while she was in charge, short of an earthquake. Even in an earthquake, thought Julia, Emily would be heroic and organised. She would know the best place to stand and take measures to ensure the survival of the merchandise. She would rally everyone around with cheery songs, like jolly ladies in underground railway stations in movies about the Blitz.

George was flattered that Emily felt 'lost without him' as he put it, although that was not exactly the way Emily had expressed it. He explained the situation apologetically to Anabel, who was very understanding. She pushed a bobby pin back into her hair and said that was perfectly all right, what if she came in the evenings instead? George was delighted and said that he would cook her dinner. So that's how it happened that Anabel became a regular dinner guest as well.

In the course of these meals, Julia discovered a lot more things about Anabel. She had trained as an English teacher, but at the moment was only working casually, which meant lots of different schools rang her up and asked her to come in when one of their teachers was pregnant or bereaved or something. She wasn't married but lived in a house in Newtown with her brother and his girlfriend. Her parents lived in the country in a town called Orange and she visited them on long weekends. Her favourite colour was green and her favourite food was pasta with cream sauce but she liked anything, really. George was her only private pupil.

Anabel brought special books to teach George with. They had photographs in them of people standing outside Big Ben in London saying things like 'Hello. My name is Juan. London is a big exciting city'. She gave George exercises for homework where he had to fill in the missing words in sentences. George tended to make wild guesses as far as these blanks were concerned, so he was not often right, but Anabel was very patient and tried to explain the rules of the language. The problem was, every time Anabel explained a rule, George would point out an example where the rule didn't apply. Then Anabel would giggle and say 'Isn't English a hopeless language?' And George would agree and say that Spanish was much more sensible, why didn't she learn Spanish, and he could teach her? At which Anabel would look doubtful and suggest they return to the textbook.

One Friday night when George cooked dinner for Anabel (fettucini with ham and cheese), Julia went to her friend Eloise's for a pyjama birthday party. They ate Kentucky Fried Chicken and custard slices and Julia felt sick and had to go and lie down in a darkened room to recover while the others played Madonna records. Eloise's mother looked in on her from time to time to see if she were all right, but Julia always pretended to be asleep, scared that Eloise's mother might make her drink salt and water or warm milk or something even more disgusting that she kept in the bathroom cupboard.

Later in the night she got up and joined the others and they all watched *Hair* on the video player. The others fell asleep at about one o'clock in the morning but Julia was still wide awake after all that resting, and watched *Dirty Dancing*, *The Karate Kid* and *Endless Love*. Just as it was getting light she fell asleep, and all the others woke up and went into the garden to play French cricket with Eloise's father.

George came and picked her up at half-past ten. Julia felt sweaty and uncomfortable, but she managed a smile for Eloise's mother and said 'Thank you for having me.' She waited wanly in the kitchen while George went and had a bat outside. After about five minutes he came back in, took Julia's hand and kissed it and said goodbye and happy birthday to Eloise. He was in a very good mood.

When he started the car he turned the radio on very loud. It was the Spanish morning on the international station and they were playing a tango about Buenos Aires. George got very sentimental and sang the words to Julia as if she were a beautiful woman in a night club. Julia closed her eyes and rested her head against the window.

'Would you like to go to the museum tomorrow?'

Julia woke with a start, banging her head on the glass. 'What?'

'The museum,' repeated George. 'Would you like to go to the museum tomorrow?'

George suddenly wound down his window and shouted something insulting in Spanish at the driver in front of him who had apparently done something wrong. George liked to insult other drivers in Spanish because he thought it made them nervous.

'What museum?' asked Julia, puzzled. She had never thought of George as a museum sort of person.

'What?' George swung the wheel round violently and hooted his horn.

'What museum?' said Julia. 'There's thousands of museums.'

'Oh, you know,' said George. 'The big museum. Near our place. Near the park. Miss Anabel suggested we might all go together tomorrow.'

'What for?' asked Julia suspiciously. 'Also Daddy, I wish you'd stop calling her Miss Anabel. It sounds silly.'

'What for?' said George, ignoring her last remark. 'What do you mean, what for? For fun, of course.'

Julia looked doubtful. She supposed it could be fun to go to a museum. 'Will Grandma come as well?'

'Of course,' said George. 'Why not?'

Julia could imagine her grandmother thinking of a few reasons why not. A nasty idea suddenly occurred to her. 'We won't have to fill in sheets, will we?' she asked anxiously. 'Or draw pictures or anything?' Julia hated filling in sheets on school excursions. She could never find anything to lean on and the ink in her biros clogged up and she always seemed to get the columns confused and had to cross everything out.

'Sheets?' said George. 'Sheets?'

Julia decided it would be kinder not to enlighten him. Poor George, he would find out soon enough. She would refuse to fill in any sheets herself, anyway. She wasn't the one learning English.

She reached in her pocket for the bag of jelly beans she'd won at a pass-the-parcel game at Eloise's party. They'd become rather squashed and warm from being sat on all night while she watched the videos. She ate a pink one and two green ones and then picked out the black ones and the purple ones that taste like medicine and put them in George's mouth while he drove. It was very convenient having a father who ate anything.

5

George and Anabel had arranged to meet on the steps outside the museum at eleven o'clock that Sunday morning. As the museum was so close to the delicatessen, George and Julia and her grandmother agreed that they would walk there – it was only about fifteen minutes away and it was a lovely blue winter day. Besides, Julia's grandmother didn't like car travel. She said the vibrations made her sick, although Julia thought it was more likely that George's driving made her sick.

To Julia's surprise, her grandmother had been quite enthusiastic about the trip to the museum. Actually, she seemed unusually fond of Anabel. She was always smiling at her and patting her on the arm – there wasn't much more she could do, seeing they didn't have a language in common. Perhaps she liked Anabel's healthy appetite. Julia had always been a disappointment to her grandmother in that way. Anabel never said no, or only sometimes to third helpings.

That morning George wore a light blue shirt with crocodile patterns on it that his sister in Adelaide had sent him for his birthday eight months before. He ate a huge omelette with parsley and spring onions for breakfast and drank three cups of hot chocolate. When Julia woke up and went out into the kitchen he said '*bellisima*' which means 'very beautiful' and picked her up and swung her into the air.

The walk to the museum ended up taking a bit longer than quarter of an hour. Julia's grandmother was naturally rather slow on her feet. She had a walking stick in one hand and held on to George with the other. She was in a good mood too, commenting in satisfied tones about how dirty the streets were, covered in rubbish, and how much nicer it was in Buenos Aires. George said yes, Buenos Aires was very nice, but some parts were pretty dirty too, just like this. His mother said what would he know, he hadn't been there for thirteen years, to which George replied she hadn't been there for ten.

George's mother changed the subject slightly then, and began reminiscing about a beautiful park where she used to take George as a baby for air, as air is very important for babies. George said yes, everyone has to breathe, don't they. At which his mother looked at him dourly and applied her walking stick to the ground with increasing force.

As they turned the corner into College Street, a priest walked by and nodded to George.

'*Baruch Hashem*,' said George nodding back, which is Hebrew for 'Blessed is God'.

'He thinks we're on our way to church,' whispered Julia, looking round at the black-frocked back, remembering it was Sunday.

'When he comes to the synagogue, I'll go to the church!' said George dramatically.

'But you never go to the synagogue,' objected Julia.

'I have to work, don't I?' George defended himself.

'Who will look after the shop if I spend all Saturday praying?'

They didn't reach the museum until quarter past eleven, which wasn't so late, really. But George was terribly worked up. Poor Anabel, to be kept waiting. Still, Anabel looked all right. She was standing next to a pink and white Mr Whippy van parked outside the museum, eating a chocolate-covered ice-cream cone. When she saw them she waved and started to gulp down the ice-cream very quickly, so that by the time they reached her only the end of the orange cone remained.

'Good morning!' said Anabel, suddenly clutching her throat with the shocked expression of someone who's just eaten something far too cold.

'G'day!' said George, slapping Anabel heartily on the back. 'Sorry we are so late.'

'Oh, that's fine,' said Anabel. 'It's a lovely morning.'

'Was the ice-cream nice?' asked Julia.

'Oh, all right,' said Anabel vaguely, as if she had already forgotten about it.

'Well,' said George, rubbing his hands together. 'So this is the museum. Twelve years in Australia and I never was here. What's inside?'

'Skeletons,' said Julia, who had been twice with her class.

'Not just skeletons,' said Anabel quickly. 'Also animals and reptiles and plants and . . .'

'So it's like a zoo?' George looked puzzled.

'No, no,' said Anabel. 'Everything's dead.'

At this point, Julia's grandmother, who had been paying a barely polite and uncomprehending attention to the conversation, announced that she would like a gelato before they went inside. George explained that Mr Whippy did not sell gelato, only soft vanilla ice-cream. Julia's grandmother sighed crankily and said she'd just seen someone with a gelato and if it hadn't come from the truck, where had it come from?

So George stood in the queue and bought four cones of mixed gelato. Julia expected Anabel might say 'Oh, no, I couldn't possibly, I've just had a chocolate-covered one', but she didn't bother. George brought back the ice-creams and they sat on the steps and ate them. At least Julia and George sat on the steps – Anabel and Julia's grandmother kept standing.

Julia's grandmother said that ice-cream was much better in Argentina. George translated this for Anabel, confessing that this was undeniably true, and that there was a particularly delicious flavour there called *dulce de leche* which he had never seen in Australia. Anabel asked if he knew the recipe because she had an ice-cream-making machine which her mother won as a lucky door prize at a Rotary club dinner-dance. George got very excited and said yes, yes, why hadn't he thought of it before? They could make litres and litres of it and sell it in the shop. People would come from miles, people would come from New Zealand just for a taste! Anabel looked doubtful and said it was a very small machine, just for the home really. But George said that was okay, he would do something to it to increase its capacity and Anabel looked more doubtful still.

Anabel was the first to finish her cone. She took a tissue from her purple string bag and tried to wipe the little smears of chocolate and rockmelon flavour from her chin. To fill in the time while the others were still eating, she told them all about her brother's girlfriend who was a curator of reptiles at the zoo. You'd think that would be an interesting job, wouldn't you, said Anabel, but all she did was complain, complain, complain. And not just about her job, either; also about the house, the food, her family – even about Anabel's brother, which Anabel thought was just going too far. After all, it's one thing to complain about your own family, but then to start attacking someone else's!

George didn't quite follow this story and his mother didn't understand it at all, but Julia thought it was interesting. She asked Anabel how her brother's girlfriend got to be a curator of reptiles, but Anabel didn't know. Then she asked Anabel why she spelled her name with only one 'n' because there were two girls at school called Annabel but they both spelled it with a double 'n'. Anabel didn't know that either – she'd never thought about it – she'd have to ask her parents. Then Julia asked how long Anabel's brother had been going out with the curator of reptiles, and Anabel sighed and said, 'Two years. It seems like a lifetime. I suppose they'll be getting married soon.'

'In a church?' asked Julia.

'Oh, I suppose so,' said Anabel wearily. 'Most people do, don't they?'

'My parents got married in a synagogue,' Julia corrected her. 'And lots of people get married in offices. Where do you want to get married?'

George stood up, swallowing the end of his cone. 'Let's go in,' he said. 'Before it closes.'

'I haven't finished my cone,' Julia complained, thinking George was being rather alarmist, seeing the museum wouldn't be closing for another four hours at least.

George clicked his tongue impatiently and told her to

throw it away, since when did she ever finish eating anything? This was true, but Julia still didn't like to waste it. So she propped up her half-eaten cone against the museum's stone fence, all its colours dripping together into a blur. Perhaps someone who wasn't very fussy about germs would come by and finish it off.

6

'Do you have a grandmother?' Julia asked Anabel as they followed George and her grandmother up the stone steps into the museum.

'No,' said Anabel. 'At least, yes, of course, everybody does, but mine are both dead.'

'Oh.' Poor Anabel. 'What about a grandfather?'

'They both died before the grandmothers. They usually do.'

What a depressing person. Julia decided not to pursue the subject of grandparents. Besides, something more urgent was bothering her.

'We don't have to fill in sheets, do we?'

'Sheets?' Anabel stood at the top of the steps looking mystified. 'What sort of sheets?'

'You know. About trilobites and continental drifts and things.' Julia paused and added meaningfully, 'I hate sheets.'

'Goodness me!' Anabel giggled and one of her bobby pins slipped out from under her fringe. 'We're here to enjoy ourselves, aren't we?'

This was not an altogether satisfactory answer, but Julia's attention was distracted by the sight of an enormous grey skeleton hanging from the ceiling. Julia loved skeletons. There was a wonderful book in the library at school, a biology book with see-through plastic pages. On the first page was a man with flesh and hair, but as you turned the pages all his layers disappeared – his skin, his muscles, his insides – until finally all that remained was his skeleton, smooth and white, which had been lying there secretly the whole time.

'What is it?' she asked Anabel, leaning her head back and gazing at the row of huge vertebrae and the curving ribs.

'It's a sperm whale,' said Anabel. 'But I don't think it's real. I mean, I think it's a copy. Made of papier mâché or something.'

'Really?' said George, suddenly looking at the skeleton with more interest and respect. 'But that's beautiful. Really beautiful work.' George was always much more impressed with man-made things than with nature.

Anabel took her pink glasses out of her bag, balanced them on her nose and read a notice positioned below the skeleton's tail. Unfortunately, it didn't offer any information about the whale but told you where the public telephones were situated.

Anabel's glasses were so scratchy and smudgy, Julia was surprised she could see through them at all. Julia wondered if she'd ever considered contact lenses. Her teacher at school, Miss Marsden, wore contact lenses – special ones that changed the colour of her eyes from brown to blue. Miss Marsden said she'd always wanted blue eyes because of Elizabeth Taylor, who didn't have blue eyes after all, she found out later.

'Well,' said Anabel. 'What would you like to see first?'

Julia's grandmother said she wanted to go and look at the museum shop. George said he hadn't come to go shopping but to get an education. Julia's grandmother said she'd had enough education to last her to the grave. Julia didn't translate this last remark for Anabel in case it sounded rude, Anabel being a teacher. In the end Julia's grandmother went off to the shop by herself while George, Julia and Anabel set off for the native fauna.

The native fauna gallery was like a series of shop windows, displaying wombats, sugar gliders and kangaroos, stuffed and furry with glass eyes, settled in amongst plastic bushes and real earth and rocks. In the middle of all these windows was a tiny cinema with soft black benches for seats. Julia sat down and watched a program all about platypuses which had a lot of diagrams and red arrows in it. When it ended, another film about rock wallabies began. Julia stood up and gave her legs a shake. She wasn't all that interested in rock wallabies. She wasn't even all that interested in platypuses, but once she'd started watching, she'd felt it would be rude to leave before the end.

Julia stepped out of the little black cinema and looked around for George and Anabel, but they didn't seem to be anywhere near by. She scanned her eyes disbelievingly up and down the length of the gallery – George would never just leave like that without saying where he was going! He never did – not even that time she'd spent twenty-five minutes looking at the embroidered cushions exhibit at the Easter Show. He'd tap his foot and look at his watch, and cough and make silly jokes and moan 'Come on' and 'Get on with it', but he never just walked off and left her alone.

Only now it very much looked like he had. Anabel, of course. Anabel must have dragged him off to look at a totem pole for a quick English lesson without another thought for her. Julia appreciated Anabel's devotion to duty, but this was so inconsiderate. And selfish. Who wanted to walk around a museum by themselves? Julia pressed the tips of her fingers against the glass pane shielding a display of a garbage bin and a stuffed pet cat, and had an impulse to punch a hole in the glass and make everyone come running to see what happened. When they asked her why she did it, she would raise a bloody finger and point it sorrowfully at George and say, 'Father Forgot Me.'

She slid her hand down the pane and put it in her pocket. It was humiliating to go and search for them, but what else could she do – apart from hiding in the toilet until after the museum closed so that George would think she had been kidnapped? And the thought of seven hours waiting all by herself in the toilet without even anything to read was not appealing. In any case, who knows, maybe George and Anabel would get so wrapped up in participles and adjectival clauses that they'd just go off together for a chocolate milkshake and forget all about her?

With a cranky shrug, Julia walked down a short flight of steps into the next gallery to look for them. It was full of scaffolding and sawdust, and there were no exhibits except for an ancient-looking diorama of an aquatic dinosaur, poking its long neck above the surface of a pond and taking a bite out of a passing bird. Julia was surprised – she had always thought dinosaurs only ate vegetables. This one must have been exceptional. It had a huge round stomach and lovely floppy flippers.

She walked quickly through an archway into another gallery, with a high ceiling and balconies along the walls with brass railings like an old-fashioned shopping arcade. On the ground level there was a long brown panel with holes where you put your eyes or your nose or your ears to find out if you were deaf or colour blind or had some other affliction. But there was no sign of George or Anabel. Julia wandered glumly along, feeling neglected. Just ahead of her was a troop of Brownie Guides, neatly dressed in brown uniforms, berets and socks. She noted with satisfaction that they were all filling in sheets.

Turning the next corner, she came face to face with a lift. For want of anything else to do, she stepped inside and pressed one of the 'up' buttons. The doors slid closed with a greasy sigh.

They opened again just as noisily to a view of the park and the cathedral through a large oblong window. Julia stepped out and leaned against the glass, staring. On one side of the street, people in white dresses were playing bowls, cars speeding down the curved road alongside them. On the other side, in the park, a man was erecting a blue and yellow tent.

'Julia.'

Julia turned around with a jump. It was her grandmother, sitting at a table with a cup of tea and a finger bun. She might have guessed it wouldn't take her grandmother long to find the cafeteria. Julia went over and sat down next to her.

'Stale,' said her grandmother in Spanish through a large mouthful of bun. 'At least five days old.'

'Did you buy anything at the shop?' asked Julia.

Her grandmother pulled her big navy-blue handbag onto the table and produced from it a see-through box filled with lots of little pieces of balsa wood that you stuck together to make a praying mantis that bobbed up and down when you touched its nose. Julia inspected it doubtfully and said that it looked a bit complicated. Her grandmother snorted and took a sip of tea. 'Absolutely disgusting,' she announced with satisfaction.

Julia looked around anxiously for the waitress, hoping that she couldn't understand Spanish, but luckily she was fully occupied speaking to someone on the telephone.

'George and Anabel went off without me,' said Julia.

'Ah,' said her grandmother.

'You haven't seen them, have you?' asked Julia.

'No,' said her grandmother.

Julia sighed and stood up. 'Do you want to come and look at an exhibition with me?'

'No,' said her grandmother.

'Well, see you later, then.'

Julia got back in the lift. She pressed another one of the buttons without much thought, and was irritated to find when she got out again that she had simply returned to the same floor she'd come from. She heard the lift chugging its way back up and considered the curving white staircase in front of her without enthusiasm.

It was then she noticed a sign in the distance saying PAPUA NEW GUINEA. That might be interesting – better than fossils, anyway, which seemed the only alternative. In the meantime, to liven things up, she decided to pretend that she was in occupied Warsaw and she'd been separated from her family in a bomb blast and now she was trying to sneak across the border. All the uniformed museum attendants could be Germans – or was it Russians they had in Warsaw? Anyway, they were the enemy.

Feeling a new purpose, she walked quickly towards the sign, past the museum shop and aboriginal fishing knives, into a series of darkened rooms. These were the unlit alleyways of Warsaw after curfew! A museum attendant smiled at her, but Julia averted her eyes in case he asked her for identity papers.

Around the corner she came to a tall triangular house,

rather like a wooden teepee, covered with long stringy leaves and painted with black and white blobs. Julia peered inside. On the floor there were mats and bowls and animalish things that might have been toys. It looked quite cosy, like camping.

'I suppose you eat and sleep in the same room,' she said to herself, delighted, forgetting for a moment the streets of occupied Warsaw. She reached out her hand and stroked the frame of the wooden house cautiously, as if it were a pony.

'Please don't touch the exhibits,' said a uniformed man, appearing suddenly from behind.

Julia froze. A German officer! She held her breath and stepped back, her heart banging. The man moved back into the shadows.

'A lucky escape!' she whispered loudly in her head, and strode onward into the darkness.

Julia was so enjoying her desperate flight in occupied Warsaw that George and Anabel had slipped into the back of her mind. That made it even more of a shock, as she hurried through a small archway, to see what she saw. She pulled herself up like a runaway horse.

In front of her was another New Guinean house – it looked like some kind of temple. It was tall and narrow and you could see right through it from one end to another, like looking down a telescope. Along the walls were strange ugly statues of gods or devils.

But it wasn't the statues that brought Julia to a halt. It was George and Anabel. George and Anabel standing in the darkness at the other end of the temple. And Anabel was kissing George.

Julia opened her mouth to say something simple like 'Hello' but only air came out. Just carbon dioxide, she thought to herself, remembering the week before's natural science class.

But George saw Julia. Very quickly he drew himself apart from Anabel. 'Oh!' he said, in an extra loud and cheerful voice. 'Hello!'

They stared at each other through the length of the temple.

'What have you been up to?' he said in Spanish.

'Nothing,' said Julia.

George came nervously down the side of the exhibit to where she was standing. Anabel slunk out from the shadows and smiled carefully at Julia. Her face was quite pink beneath the freckles.

'Hello!' she said, not so brightly. 'We lost you.'

Julia did not reply. Anabel looked at George and then down at the ground. She frowned suddenly, then bent down and picked up a rusty bobby pin.

'Are you sure it's yours?' enquired Julia coldly. 'You might get nits.'

'Oh.' Anabel dropped the pin and giggled. She looked at George again, but he was smiling at Julia, his hand on his head.

'Excuse me,' said Julia, shaking off his hand. 'I've got to go to the toilet.'

She walked away from them as quickly as she could without being told not to run by one of the attendants. She went straight out of the New Guinea gallery, past the museum shop and down the grubby stone steps right out of the museum itself.

Julia stood at the bottom of the steps, biting her thumbnail. Her unfinished ice-cream was still there, propped up against the railing, just as she had left it, except that the ice-cream had all melted and turned into a

41

thick brown puddle, going hard and sticky in the sun.

She sat down on the last step, trembling. How could such a thing happen? Her own father! Julia reached into her pocket and pulled out a five-cent piece and started scraping the step with it. She knew it wasn't a very nice thing to do, but she would rather have done something much worse. How could he? How could she? How could anybody?

Julia felt something very much like tears forming themselves in the space in the back of her head. She shook her head roughly. She didn't want to cry – she hardly knew what she wanted to do. She felt like running across the road to where the people were putting up the tent, and talking to someone she'd never seen before – pretending she was a completely different person, and then just disappearing.

'There you are!'

Julia quickly pocketed the five-cent piece and swung around. George stood at the top of the steps with her grandmother and Anabel, unsmiling.

'We were waiting for you!' he said reproachfully. 'Why didn't you tell us you were going outside?'

Julia stood up, muttering. She would have liked to counter that she was not the only one who went off without telling people where they were going. But at the sight of her father, she was suddenly overcome by a terrible pity for George, and the situation he had fallen into. George was like a child. Julia remembered with a shiver Anabel's innocent stare halfway through her glasses, and that terrible giggle. Poor George, he didn't know what he was doing.

She climbed the stairs two by two, and with her back to Anabel, took hold of his hand and began to pull him along. 'I think we should go home now,' she said firmly.

'Oh!' said George, then, after a pause, 'All right then.'
Julia managed a rather grim smile. She would show
Anabel that George wasn't the sort of man to be con-
quered with a kiss. But even as they came down the stairs
together she was struck by a terrible thought – what if it
weren't Anabel who had kissed George, but George who
had kissed Anabel?

7

The next day at school, during eleven o'clock recess, Julia told her friend Eloise all about George and Anabel. To Julia's disappointment, Eloise was not particularly shocked or outraged. 'Much worse things happen on TV,' she pointed out sensibly. 'At least George and Anabel aren't married to other people.'

'But George was married,' said Julia. 'To my mother.'

'Well, people do get married more than once, you know,' said Eloise with a worldly sigh. 'Elizabeth Taylor's been married seven times.'

They knew all about Elizabeth Taylor from Miss Marsden. It was cold comfort. Julia rammed her hands into the pockets of her blazer and felt the holes in the bottom corners.

'Wouldn't you like George to marry again at all?' asked Eloise curiously. 'Wouldn't you like to have a mother?'

'What for?' snapped Julia, trying to picture Anabel as a mother.

'Oh well.' Eloise searched for an answer. 'Well my mother takes me to swimming lessons after school.'

Even Julia, who had no personal experience of

mothers, felt there must be more to it than that. But she said nothing, swinging around in a circle on the ball of her foot.

'*Solamente una vez*,' sang George soulfully that evening, as he dished out rice and eggs into Julia's bowl and then her grandmother's.

'Aren't you eating?' asked Julia, looking at him strangely. George always ate more dinner than both of them put together.

'I'm on a diet!' George announced proudly, slapping his stomach with the palm of his hand. 'I have to think of my health.'

'Life is short – live it up!' retorted Julia's grandmother. 'Your father never went on a diet in his life.'

Julia's mouth was hanging open in disbelief. 'You have to think of my health,' she repeated, astounded. George never thought of his health without prompting.

Julia's grandmother patted her arm. 'He's not thinking of his health,' she said. 'He's thinking of his figure and his new girlfriend.'

His new girlfriend! thought Julia savagely. She obviously never worries about her figure, so why should George?

'Anabel likes to eat, doesn't she?' said Julia, to no one in particular.

'Ah, Anabel.' George's face softened.

'You have to eat,' said Julia's grandmother firmly. 'A working man has to eat.'

'I suppose I will have to eat eventually,' George agreed.

'It's not as if rice and eggs are unwholesome,' continued Julia's grandmother.

'No,' said George.

Julia's grandmother took a third bowl and dealt out a large helping. She pushed the bowl towards him.

'Oh well,' said George, avoiding Julia's eyes.

Julia stood up quickly and left the table. She went into the kitchen and turned the hot water tap on over the remains in her dinner bowl. Her thoughts were rapid, angry and unhappy, and she felt a headache rising as the steam from the tap gathered about her in a hot cloud. She didn't know what to do. She didn't know how to help. Normally it was so easy to explain things to George. He would ask her advice and look at her with respect and boast to his friends about how he consulted her in everything. But now when he was really in trouble he was telling her nothing. He hadn't said a word to her about what happened in the museum. He just smiled and babbled on in his normal way, as if nothing were the matter. And all the while Anabel was tightening her grip and it would get harder and harder to extricate him . . .

On Wednesday night, Anabel came around as usual to give George his English lesson. The shop had been very busy that day, and George and Emily were still hard at work cleaning up, counting the money and getting things ready for the morning. So Anabel waited in the living room for him to come upstairs.

Julia was sitting on the sofa, watching a TV program about fish. Her grandmother was having a bath, and the sound of her swishing the water around the bathtub came eerily into the living room as the tropical fish on the television swam in and out of the coral reef.

Anabel smiled tentatively at Julia and sat down in an armchair. Julia fixed her eyes on the fish. Anabel reached into her bag and pulled out a packet of what smelt like barley sugar. Bits of paper wrappers scattered about the floor.

'Oh dear,' said Anabel, and she knelt down to pick them up.

She probably hasn't emptied her bag in five years, thought Julia in disgust, watching Anabel out of the corner of her eye.

Anabel took the various bits of paper out to the rubbish bin in the kitchen.

'Do you mind if I make myself a cup of coffee?' she called out.

Julia grunted a non-committal reply. She heard Anabel fill the kettle and light the gas. Anabel then came back into the living room and sat down again. 'A watched pot never boils,' she said feebly.

'It'd have to, in the end,' Julia remarked, hoping that Anabel might go back into the kitchen to see it happen. But Anabel only relaxed back into the chair and said, 'I've been dying for a cup of coffee all day. I've been relief teaching, you see, at Avalon, and it's so far away that I have to get up and leave the house without having time for breakfast. And then in the staffroom they only had herbal teas because the school's having an anti-drug week and no one's meant to have caffeine or cigarettes, only I'm sure one of the teachers was smoking because there was a definite smell in the corridor at morning tea. Although I suppose it could have been one of the students,' said Anabel thoughtfully. 'After all, the anti-drug week was the teachers' idea, not the students', so you couldn't really expect them to be so scrupulous. Of course, it's completely forbidden for the students to smoke,' she added, her voice taking on a note of authority.

Julia's eyes remained focused on the fish. The kettle

began to whistle. Anabel dashed to the kitchen in a fluster, saying as she went, 'Help yourself to a barley sugar.'

Julia sneaked a look down at the open packet lying on the coffee table. She wished barley sugar did not come in such crackly wrappings, as she would have liked to take one but didn't want Anabel to hear.

Anabel came back, stirring a mug of coffee with the sugar spoon.

'If you put that back in the sugar bowl,' Julia observed, 'the sugar'll go all brown and lumpy.'

'Oh dear, sorry,' giggled Anabel. Some coffee splashed onto her hands and shirt. Sucking her fingers, she sat down on the sofa next to Julia. 'I suppose I shouldn't have sugar at all,' she apologised.

'Pure, white and deadly,' agreed Julia, remembering something she'd read in a pamphlet at the dentist.

The door swung open, and George came in, sweaty and smiling. He strode over to Anabel, beaming, and took her hand. For one horrifying moment, Julia thought he was going to kiss her again, but, perhaps catching her eye, he stopped just in time.

'Fine! Fine!' he said with a grin, although no one had asked him how he was.

'Anabel's been relief teaching at Avalon,' Julia informed him.

'Goodness me!' said George in his best English voice, as if this were something particularly admirable.

'Yes I've just been telling Julia –' Anabel began, but George interrupted her, saying to Julia in Spanish, 'Do turn off the television, my love. I can hardly hear Miss Anabel speak.'

Julia crawled across the floor to the television and switched it off, thinking to herself that the noise of the fish was nothing compared to 'Magnum' or 'The A Team' or any of the other awful programs that George used to watch before he started taking English lessons.

'. . . that I've been dying for a cup of coffee all day . . .' continued Anabel, nervously looking at Julia and finding herself unable to say any more.

'I must have a shower before the studies,' George announced, breaking the short silence. 'I will be very quick.'

'The bathroom's occupied,' said Julia. 'And you know how long she takes.'

'Isn't your mother rather old to have a bath by herself?' said Anabel in a concerned voice. 'She might slip. My grandmother did.'

'Was it a fatal slip?' asked Julia, interested.

'I put a special bar,' said George hurriedly. 'You know, for holding. Special modifications. To be independent.'

'Oh well, yes, independence is very important,' said Anabel, sounding like a teacher. 'Hamsters, for example, have to be kept alone. They only tolerate each other briefly for mating.'

The word 'hamster' was beyond George's vocabulary, and Julia was not in the mood for translating, so he just smiled at her adoringly and said, 'Oh yes, of course. True.' Then, 'How about a beer?' He had learnt that she was not very fond of tea.

'Oh! Thank you,' said Anabel.

'What about anti-drugs week?' Julia reminded her.

'Oh well.' Anabel swept anti-drugs week aside. 'I'm sure it doesn't apply after hours. That would be an infringement of personal liberties.'

Julia sighed and went to her bedroom. She lay down on the bed and stared at the ceiling. She tried to think of something nice she could tell Eloise about Anabel

49

tomorrow, but it was impossible. The worst part was, she had only herself to blame. If only she hadn't seen that notice in the newsagent window. If only she hadn't rung that number. If only her courage had failed her at the last moment as it very nearly had. Julia groaned and rolled over.

She could hear two men out on the street, having a ferocious argument over where one of them wanted to park his car. Julia imagined one of them taking a knife to the other and stabbing him to death. Then she would be a witness – an ear-witness, they'd call it. She'd have to testify in court and the murderer would glare at her with loathing and she would get death threats from his relatives and crime partners and have to have twenty-four hour police protection.

Disappointingly, the two men suddenly seemed to come to an agreement and were even laughing. Perhaps they'd only been pretending to be angry after all. People do that quite a lot, she thought, sitting up. George, for example, was often shouting at Emily about some disaster or other, but all the time his eyes were laughing.

She could hear him laughing now, followed by Anabel's interminable giggle. Her grandmother must have finally finished her bath, because she could hear her offering Anabel something to eat in Spanish, and George's not very precise translations.

Julia switched on her bedside light and pulled out a Bible she had bought at a flower show. She'd decided to read the whole thing all the way through, even the New Testament, by her thirteenth birthday. So far, she had only got halfway through the book of Exodus and she wasn't finding it very interesting. She stared down at the page.

Fifty loops shalt thou make in one curtain, and fifty loops shalt thou make in the edge of the curtain that is in the coupling of the second; that the loops may take hold of one another.

Reading something like this made Julia wonder if perhaps it mightn't be better to be an atheist like Eloise. Eloise had never read the Bible – her parents wouldn't allow a copy in the house. When Eloise went to hospital to have her appendix out, her father wrote NA in the column of her registration paper marked RELIGION. The nurse had asked what church this was and Eloise's father had had to explain that it meant Not Applicable.

The door of Julia's room opened and George's head poked around. 'I'm making pancakes,' he said. 'Would you like to come out and have some?'

'No thank you,' said Julia. 'I'm busy.'

'Oh come on,' said George, sitting on the bed beside her. 'You can't spend all your time reading. Your eyes'll fall out.'

'That's very unlikely,' replied Julia firmly. 'Anyway, two days ago you were on a diet.'

George laughed and pinched her cheek. Julia's head remained bent towards Exodus.

'Okay, then.' George shrugged and stood up. 'I'll save some for you and put it in the fridge.'

He went out, closing the door behind him, and Julia found herself smiling in spite of it all. Only George would suggest something like that. What could be more disgusting than cold pancakes?

8

Three and a half weeks later, Anabel issued an invitation. 'I'd like you to come and have lunch at my house,' she said to George. 'My parents are down from the country and my brother will be there too, of course.'

'And the curator of reptiles?' asked Julia, who was lying on the floor of the living room reading a magazine.

'Oh yes,' said Anabel, with a marked drop in enthusiasm.

'*Encantado*!' declared George gallantly, referring to the invitation. (This means 'delighted' in Spanish.)

'And Julia and your mother too,' said Anabel, leaning over and patting Julia's hand.

'What a lot of food you'll have to cook,' said Julia, carefully removing her arm.

'Oh well.' Anabel looked ashamed. 'Actually, my brother's girlfriend will probably do the cooking. She's done a course in France and everything.'

'In France,' repeated George, impressed.

'And everything,' repeated Julia, thoughtfully. Perhaps that included training to be a curator of reptiles.

The lunch was on a Sunday, of course, because that

was when the shop was closed, They had to drive as it was too far to walk, and even Julia's grandmother preferred George's driving to the bus. It was a particularly wet day – the rain sloshed against the windscreen as if they were in an automatic car wash. George swore and said he couldn't see anything and they were sure to run into the back of a semi-trailer. Julia's grandmother silently clung onto the edges of her seat.

Anabel must have been looking out for them, because just as they were parking outside her house, she appeared at the front door and shouted, 'Do you have an umbrella?'

Of course they'd all forgotten theirs, so Anabel went back inside the house and came out again with a small broken spotty one.

'Better than nothing,' she said optimistically, although it wasn't, really, as by the time they'd all been ferried inside they were as soggy as bathmats and had to shake themselves off like dogs after a swim.

Standing in the hallway were a man and a woman, who looked older than George but not as old as his mother. The man was in a brown safari suit and the woman in a crimson dress. They both wore glasses.

'These are my parents,' explained Anabel.

'Pleased to meet you!' said George, shaking hands enthusiastically.

'This is George,' continued Anabel, 'and George's mother and his daughter, Julia.'

Julia's grandmother smiled unconvincingly, as she was still recovering from the rain and the drive. Julia felt too young to shake hands so she gave a little bow.

'Well,' giggled Anabel, 'let's go in and sit down.'

She led them into a large, dark and not very tidy living

room, with a floppy floral sofa in it and matching armchairs. Julia found an orange vinyl beanbag in a corner and knelt down into it while the others arranged themselves amongst the lounge suite.

'Well!' said Anabel, for the thirtieth time. 'What a terrible day!'

'Terrible,' agreed George immediately. 'Extremely terrible.'

'It's worse in Orange,' observed Anabel's father, whose name was Mr Sedlon.

'It's always worse in Orange,' sighed Anabel, 'no matter what you're talking about.'

'What about a cool drink, Anabel?' suggested Mrs Sedlon, Anabel's mother. 'Your guests must be thirsty after their trip.'

Julia stifled a giggle. Anabel's mother made it sound as if they'd just ridden camelback through a dusty desert. But before Anabel could answer, a tall girl with a long black plait dressed in blue jeans and a yellow jumper came into the room, carrying a circular tin tray of glasses of orange juice.

'Good afternoon,' said the girl graciously.

She had an American accent. This must be the curator of reptiles, thought Julia.

'Patrice, my brother's fiancée,' explained Anabel.

'How do you do?' said Patrice. 'Would you care for a juice?'

Patrice was so clean and cool, a bit like a lizard herself.

'Luncheon will be ready soon,' mentioned Patrice. 'Michael is in the kitchen warming the plates.'

Something in the kitchen fell to the floor with a crash.

'If you'll just excuse me,' said Patrice in her gracious monotone.

'Lovely girl,' remarked Mr Sedlon, after she had left the room.

'Very tall,' said George non-committally, as he preferred Anabel.

'American,' said Mrs Sedlon. 'Americans are tall, I believe.'

'But I am American,' said George, 'and I am short.'

'I thought you were from Argentina,' said Mrs Sedlon, puzzled.

'South America!' returned George triumphantly. 'So I am also American.'

'Oh, but when we say American, we mean the United States of America,' explained Mr Sedlon in a slow clear voice to George, who was perfectly well aware of the fact.

'Well he's still short,' said Julia, who wanted to support George.

'Not all that short,' objected Anabel. 'I never think of George as short.'

'Not, however, as tall as Americans,' insisted Mr Sedlon.

This unfortunate conversation looked as if it were going to repeat itself. To Julia's relief, Patrice appeared at the doorway and announced, 'Luncheon is served.'

'Luncheon' consisted of pumpkin soup with toast, followed by chicken salad. Although Anabel was supposed to be the hostess, she acted more like one of the guests, with that expectant, polite look that people get on their faces when they have no idea what's going to happen next.

Anabel never got around to introducing her brother, but as everyone knew who he must be, it didn't really matter. He wasn't at all like Anabel – very quiet, thin and pale, as he scuttled in and out of the kitchen with plates of food.

'Why have you come to Sydney?' George asked Anabel's parents conversationally, halfway through the pumpkin soup.

'Army business,' said Mr Sedlon importantly, wiping his mouth with a napkin.

Julia's eyes widened. Anabel's father was in the army?

'Salvation Army,' explained Mrs Sedlon quickly, although this explanation did not enlighten George. 'We're not officers, of course. Just simple soldiers.'

'Salvation Army?' George raised his eyebrows.

'It's a kind of church,' said Anabel. 'They've come for a conference – you know, a meeting.'

'Oh.' George looked admiringly across at Mr and Mrs Sedlon. 'A meeting.'

'Mum and Dad met in the Army,' said Anabel. 'Officer training school.'

'Yes, we were going to be officers,' sighed Mrs Sedlon nostalgically. 'Caused quite a scandal when we dropped out.'

'Why did you drop out?' asked Julia curiously.

'The Lord had other plans,' said Mr Sedlon in a mysterious voice.

'Alfred wanted to start his own business,' revealed Mrs Sedlon. 'Chicken farming.'

'I also escaped the army,' volunteered George. 'In Argentina. They wanted to send me to Patagonia.'

'Dear me!' said Mrs Sedlon, shocked. 'Patagonia. How unpleasant. How did you ... er ... escape?'

'Oh, my uncle paid a lot of money,' said George casually.

There was a short silence.

'Dear me!' repeated Mrs Sedlon eventually.

'The fascism,' explained George. 'It's not possible,

56

you understand. So they gave me another job. Driving. I was chauffeur for a general. Terrible. So much driving. Night and day, one girlfriend to the other, all in different states.'

Anabel giggled. So did Julia, unintentionally catching Anabel's eye.

'Well,' said Mr Sedlon, clearing his throat. 'I suppose life in Argentina must be very colourful. Exciting.'

'Exciting?' said George, surprised. 'No, the opposite. Depressing. I like Australia. Here you have the beach, right in the city.'

'Well, certainly, that's an advantage,' agreed Mrs Sedlon. 'But of course, we live in the country. Have you visited our countryside?' she asked, turning to Julia's grandmother who was demolishing a large plate of potato salad.

'Perdon?' Julia's grandmother smiled.

'My mother's English,' George apologised. 'She doesn't speak yet.'

'Oh please don't mention it,' said Mrs Sedlon.

And how's your Spanish? thought Julia defensively. Why should George have to apologise for his mother's English?

There was no dessert, as Patrice didn't believe in cakes or dairy products, but there was fresh fruit in the living room and jasmine tea. Patrice became a lot more talkative now that the main part of the meal was over, and Julia was able to ask her all about being a curator of reptiles. She received a series of highly informative answers, rather like a textbook, in reply.

'Do you ever see any of the other animals? Besides reptiles?' asked Julia in desperation after Patrice finished reeling off a description of her typical day, which seemed to consist entirely of log books, interviews and feed experiments.

'You mean mammals?' said Patrice, without enthusiasm.

'Well, yes,' said Julia, 'like kangaroos and koalas and wombats and things.'

'They have popular appeal, of course,' admitted Patrice, 'but I am not really very interested in mammals, least of all placental mammals, I'm afraid. But I realise that's what most people want to see.'

'Some reptiles have popular appeal,' objected Julia. 'What about crocodiles? I bet heaps of people want to see the crocodiles.'

'Crocodiles are the exception.'

'Or alligators,' suggested Julia. 'Or turtles.'

'Yes, well, there are several exceptions.'

Patrice stood up and offered Julia's grandmother some paw-paw. Perhaps she only expected her to take one piece, because she looked rather taken aback when she took the whole plate out of her hands.

It wasn't until they were standing up ready to go that George remembered to give Anabel the box of chocolates with the red and gold wrappers and pictures of Mozart on them that he had brought for her. He also gave her a kiss. Anabel blushed.

'Well isn't that nice!' said Mrs Sedlon.

'She always had a sweet tooth,' said Mr Sedlon, slapping Anabel heartily on the back. He bent down and whispered loudly in Julia's ear, 'It'll be wedding bells for these two before long – you mark my words.'

It was as though the whisper froze in Julia's ear, because she heard it over and over again on the way home in the car, and later still as she lay in bed that night, trying to sleep. Wedding bells? Impossible. It couldn't be. Could it?

And all she could see in reply was Anabel's blush and George's kind adoring eyes.

9

Anabel.

Julia groaned, staring up at the ceiling as she lay in bed the next morning, listening to her grandmother move dishes about the kitchen. Anabel. Chocolates. Glasses falling off. Bobby pins. Wedding bells? Oh Anabel. Julia squeezed her thin knees up over her chest and closed her eyes.

Of course, the first thing she thought of was murder. Julia had already read eleven Agatha Christie books, so she knew all about murder. She and Eloise used to rate how good the story was by the number of bodies in it – the highest they had read so far was four, but Eloise's mother said she had read one with at least ten.

The only problem with murderers in stories was that they always got found out in the end – even the cleverest ones. Julia definitely did not want to get found out. George might never want to see her again and they might hang her high from the gallows, although she knew there weren't gallows any more. But they might think she was so evil they'd send her to America to the electric chair and she'd have to live in Death Row with all those other awful murderers she'd seen pictures of on the television. Watching the second hand on her alarm clock ticking around the dial, Julia wondered if murder might not be the best way to deal with the problem.

But was it the only way? How else do you get rid of people like Anabel who don't want to go? It was easy to get rid of them temporarily – in books, you just sent them a telegram saying their aunt was ill, or you gave them free tickets to a concert and that night you robbed their house, or you just called them away to the telephone, if it was for a very short time. But none of these measures would be any use with Anabel – she would just keep coming back, hungry as ever.

Julia got out of bed and opened the top drawer in her wardrobe. She considered wearing the yellow socks that George's sister had brought her back from Disneyland. She also considered asking her friend Eloise for advice. Eloise knew lots about lots of things – but could she be trusted? Murderers should never have accomplices; they must work silent, sneaky and alone.

Julia's grandmother walked with her to school that morning – to get fresh air, she said. Not that there was any fresh air where they lived, just the smell of buses and trucks and garbage rotting in the gutters and breezes of bread baking and strong coffee. They didn't talk as they walked. Julia was thinking too hard, staring at her feet, and her grandmother didn't seem to be in the mood for chatting.

When they reached the school gate, Julia's grandmother kissed her on both cheeks more tenderly than usual and gave her a funny look.

'Everything all right?' she said in Spanish.

'Sure,' said Julia uneasily, wondering if her

grandmother could see murder in her eyes. She looked about her, up at the statue in the school yard of a khaki-clothed soldier with his arm broken off. 'Why not?'

'Ah.' Julia's grandmother smiled and stroked her head. 'See you later.'

She started to hobble back down Crown Street. Julia watched her for a moment, fearing a great gust of wind or a boy on a skateboard might suddenly come by and knock her over. She tried to imagine feeling so weak. When George lifted her up in the air and swung her around she felt very weak and frail. Poor Grandmother – for her, the whole world must seem like George's thick, strong arms.

When she got home that afternoon, Anabel was there as usual, but Julia now looked at her in a different light. She began to consider Anabel's potential as a victim. 'The victim is the key to the crime' – that was what the detectives always said.

First, who would benefit from Anabel's death? She didn't imagine that Anabel had much money – if she did, you'd think she might buy herself a new pair of glasses. Of course, she could be an eccentric millionaire who was very stingy. Julia had read a story in the afternoon paper about someone like that who never went out, and lived off jelly and instant custard, always being very particular to buy the cheapest brand.

But she didn't think she should count on Anabel secretly having stacks of money in her house in Newtown to provide someone else with a motive. Who would she leave it to, anyway? Probably her brother, and no detective could possibly suspect him of murder – he didn't even speak. Patrice was a different matter. She could hide a poisonous snake she brought home in a paper bag from work under Anabel's pillow, that could slither out and bite her while she was sleeping, or Patrice could put a boa constrictor in the drawer with Anabel's socks so that when she opened it in the morning she would get a shock and drop down dead from a heart attack so it wouldn't even have to squeeze her to death. Patrice could just say that she put the boa there to keep it warm because the temperature control in its cage had gone funny. The perfect murder.

'Do you mind if I turn on the TV?' asked Anabel, smiling up at Julia's serious face.

Julia shivered. What if Anabel were clairvoyant and could read her mind? Then she might write down in her diary everything Julia was planning and the police would find it amongst her papers after her death and come and take Julia into custody.

'No, that's fine,' she replied casually, trying not to look suspicious.

Anabel switched on the television and settled down in an armchair. George was still downstairs, fixing up the shop's books. Julia slid sideways onto the sofa and pretended to watch the screen. She started to organise her thoughts through an elimination process, like Miss Marsden had taught them in maths.

First, she obviously couldn't shoot Anabel. She couldn't get hold of a gun, and anyway, she didn't know how to use one and it would make such a loud noise that everyone would come running and catch her in the act. Unless she managed to entice Anabel away to a lonely forest and jumped out from behind a ten thousand-year-old tree with a huge wide trunk, like she'd seen in an Alfred Hitchcock movie. But how would she get to the lonely forest in the first place? She'd have to get a taxi which would cost more money than she had, and the taxi driver would remember her face and identify her in a line-up.

She couldn't push her out a window either – Anabel was so much bigger and heavier: Julia wouldn't be able to budge her. Even if she started training at the gym, it would take her so long to get enough muscles that George and Anabel would be married and on their honeymoon before she got a chance to try out her strength. And she could hardly strangle her either because she wasn't tall enough to reach her neck. Perhaps electrocution? But knowing her, she would probably frizzle herself in the process. Julia sighed. It was a wonder anyone ever got murdered at all, there were so many difficulties.

Julia sneaked a sideways look at Anabel. She was rubbing her eyes under her glasses and she looked very tired. Such a busy life Anabel led, rushing off to this school and that school. Then rushing to the delicatessen to teach George, then rushing home to rake up the leaves in her back garden at Newtown or help her brother with the washing up. No wonder her clothes were always dirty and coming to bits. She needed a rest. Really, to murder her would almost be doing her a favour.

Poison!

She would have to poison her. It was ideal.

Once it had occurred to her, Julia realised there was no other choice. Lots of things in the world were poisonous – they had learnt about it at school. And at any rate, poison would mean that Anabel would have a peaceful death. She'd just go to sleep and not wake up. 'Died peacefully at home' – that's what people put in the papers about their relatives and it was meant to be a nice thing to say. Anabel would just do it a bit earlier than normal, that's all.

Having decided to poison Anabel, Julia relaxed a little. Now that she knew Anabel wasn't going to be around much longer, she could even pity her. In fact, she tried to be as nice as possible, which made George happy, although she noticed her grandmother looking at her strangely from time to time.

Julia spent several lunchtimes in the school library reading about poisons in the Encyclopaedia Britannica. It ended up taking more time than perhaps was necessary, because, as she didn't want anyone to know what she was doing, every time somebody approached her table, she would quickly flip over the pages and immerse herself in subjects such as Polish Literature or Proboscidea. By the time she'd read a few lines of it, she couldn't help but get interested and want to read more, and then the bell would ring, and she couldn't get started on Poisons again until the next day.

Even then, it took a lot of heavy ploughing through not very exciting paragraphs about toxicology until Julia finally found something practical about murder. It wasn't much:

> Before the advance of forensic toxicology, murder by poisoning was an attractive method for disposing of one's enemies, rivals, and other objects of passion without fear of being found out. Although today this is less common, homicidal poisoning is by no means non-existent in modern society.

What was Anabel, she wondered – an enemy, a rival or an object of passion? She was certainly George's object of passion, although anyone who'd ever met Anabel might find it difficult to identify her with those words. But reading on, Julia was irritated and astonished to find that was all the encyclopaedia had to offer on the subject of murder by poisoning. She could hardly believe it. Nothing about the best and worst methods, where to get poisons, which were the hardest to trace. Nothing!

Julia banged the book shut. Hopeless. So many of these sorts of books were disappointments, and not just on the subject of murder. Volumes and volumes of pages and pages of the thinnest paper with the smudgiest smallest writing and the darkest nastiest pictures, and still nothing that you really needed to know.

'Can I help you, Julia?'

Julia's eyes shot up, startled. Thank goodness she had closed the book. Miss Marsden's bright, not-so-Elizabeth-Taylor eyes gazed helpfully down at her.

'You look rather hot and bothered,' said Miss Marsden. 'Perhaps I can help you find what you want.'

'It's okay, I think,' said Julia, standing up, clutching the encyclopaedia in one hand and pulling up her socks with the other.

'Is this something for class?' enquired Miss Marsden.

'Oh no, I was just interested,' said Julia, swinging around wildly in her mind for a word, 'in toxicology,' she finished, pleased, sure that Miss Marsden would not know what she meant.

'Oh! Poisons!' Miss Marsden laughed. 'What a funny thing for a little girl to want to read about.'

'Are you getting married?' asked Julia, desperately changing the subject, pointing at a ring on Miss Marsden's finger that she'd only started wearing two weeks ago.

Miss Marsden turned pink and looked slightly ill. 'Well, eventually, I hope,' she said in a cooler tone. 'I think perhaps you should go outdoors now, Julia, and get some fresh air. It certainly can't do you any good sitting inside all lunchtime reading about poisons.'

Perhaps it would be easier to push Anabel out the window, thought Julia that night as she ate dinner (beetroot and sour cream with dill) sitting opposite Anabel, who was trying to suck cream from her hair.

'I am getting sticky,' giggled Anabel.

'Poor Anabel,' said Julia kindly. Her grandmother looked sharply at her.

'Perhaps you should wear a hat while you eat,' Julia suggested. 'I've got a Brownie beret you could stick it all under. Like doctors, you know.'

'But then we would not see Anabel's beautiful hair,' objected George. 'So beautiful. The colour of . . . of a river.'

It would have to be a particularly muddy river, thought Julia, but she didn't say anything.

'It's nice, isn't it?' continued George, beaming around the table at them, 'all having dinner together.'

Anabel blushed. Julia's grandmother raised her eyebrows, which generally meant yes. Julia took another mouthful of beetroot.

'All together,' George repeated, sighing happily. 'All the family.'

Julia went to bed very early that night. She realised she had a lot of planning to do and she could no longer afford to lose any time. 'All the family'. What a thud fell in her heart when George said that. After she got into her pyjamas, she took out her rainbow pad, ruled a line down one side and wrote:

Where?
When?
Why?
What?
How?

She considered writing in a secret code or at least in invisible ink. She could get some lemon juice from the kitchen and put it inside her special calligraphy pen. But she didn't want to go to the kitchen. She was sure George and Anabel were kissing in the living room, or George was falling asleep on Anabel's lap in front of the television, and she'd rather not see. She decided to write it in ordinary ink and eat it when she had finished. Then it would remain inside her, destroyed and semi-digested, like a mysterious blood pact.

She started to write.

Where? ???
When? ???
Why?   Obvious reasons
What?   ??????
How?   Poison

She decided that the 'What' was silly (what was What?), and she scratched it out. Then she scratched out 'Why' because she knew very well why and she didn't need to write it down. Then she crossed out the 'Poison' after 'How' because it was too vague.

Julia looked down at the pink crumpled page. It was hardly worth eating, really. Instead she tore it off the pad, folded it and tucked it away in her red plastic wallet, along with Grant Event's bus pass. It would be just as well to have it handy in case she had a sudden inspiration.

In the middle of that night, long after Anabel went home, inspiration did come to Julia. She woke up feeling hot, and tossed the blanket on the floor. She got up and padded through the house to the toilet in her bare feet. The floor of the bathroom was cold and still wet from George's shower. Julia stared down at the little orange and tan tiles in a half-asleep stupor.

Of course! She almost said it out loud. She knew the 'How'! What did Anabel like doing more than anything in the world? What did Anabel never say no to? What would be a million times easier than injecting her with a hypodermic syringe, or putting thalium in her shaving cream, or spiking her with a blow dart from the Amazon Basin? (These were the poisoning methods she knew from books.) Food! She would poison her food! Julia remembered that Miss Marsden had said once that even peanut butter sandwiches could poison you if you ate enough of them. Of course, it might be difficult to get Anabel to eat that many peanut butter sandwiches, but there must be easier things. She would make some especially delicious food that Anabel would eat tonnes and tonnes of and then just fall asleep and they wouldn't ever hear from her again.

Julia splashed her face with tap water, now so excited she didn't feel at all like going back to sleep. She scampered back to her room, turned on her bedside light and took out the sheet of rainbow paper from her wallet. Next to 'How' she wrote:

How? Poison her dinner

That mightn't be exactly what she'd end up doing, but it was enough for now. Julia grinned to herself, pulled off her hot flannelette pyjamas and put on a summer nightie instead. Her brain was ticking over with satisfaction. She even managed to think, Poor old Anabel, she really wasn't so bad. She wondered if George would let her go to the funeral. Would George go to the funeral?

Suddenly, strangely, George's face, wet and soft, like it sometimes was on her birthday, came into her mind. Julia frowned and shook her head hard, as if to shake him away. She picked up a book on cheese-making in Greece from her bedside table and started to read it. But the pictures of Greek cows and vats of curd gave way to George's eyes, staring sadly at her. She turned off the light and pulled her pillow over her head, determined to fall asleep.

10

Only two days later, Anabel fell down in the garden and broke her ankle. Julia was at home alone when Patrice rang up with the news.

'How did she fall down in the garden?' asked Julia, puzzled.

'She was digging up weeds,' said Patrice, 'and she slipped into an old fish pond. We didn't know it was there, you see.'

'You mean a fish pond, still with water and fish?' said Julia.

'Well, not any more. Not for some years, I would say. Although I noticed some unusual aquatic helminths at the bottom. Worms, you know. I took some samples, of course.'

Julia preferred not to pursue the subject of aquatic worms. 'Is she in hospital?'

'Oh yes,' said Patrice. 'We called the ambulance, as I only had my motorbike and Anabel wasn't very keen. She became almost hysterical, actually. Virtually screamed for the police rescue squad.'

Julia tried to imagine Anabel being winched up into a

helicopter with a strap around her stomach, waving for-lornly down at Patrice as she was carried off into the sky.

'She'll be in hospital for at least a week,' said Patrice. 'In St Vincents. They had to put a pin in and she's all stuck up in plaster. Anyway, just before she went under the anaesthetic, she asked me to call George.'

'Oh.' Julia rolled her eyes. It sounded painfully romantic.

'So you'll let him know, won't you? I can't keep chatting. I must take a look at these helminths before they dehydrate.'

'Okay. Bye.'

Patrice didn't say goodbye but just hung up. Julia looked at her watch. Four o'clock. George was out buying herrings. He was very fussy about his herrings and would only buy them from one person who only sold them at one time on one day of the month. George wouldn't be back till six, smelling sweaty and fishy, complaining and very happy.

Julia went downstairs slowly to the shop, where Emily and her grandmother looked as if they were almost having a conversation. When they saw Julia they both fell silent, and so Julia of course guessed they had been talking, or trying to talk, about her. And Anabel, she wondered? Well now she could really give them something to talk about.

'Anabel's had a terrible accident and she's in hospital,' she announced, first in English and then in Spanish.

'Oh my God!' said Julia's grandmother, seizing Julia's wrist.

'Oh dear,' said Emily more stoically. 'That's no good, is it? What happened?' (Emily was used to people having accidents.)

'She fell in a fish pond,' said Julia, drawing it out.

'That's nasty,' said Emily. 'I bet her clothes smell bad.'

'And she broke her ankle,' Julia finished, in Spanish and English, unable to hold out any more.

Julia's grandmother released her grip a little. 'When? How? Where?' she demanded, and 'We must tell George.'

'We can wait till he gets back, can't we?' said Julia. 'She's not dying or anything. About telling George,' she explained to Emily in English.

'I think George would want to know as soon as possible,' said Emily, masterful as ever. 'I'd give him a ring if I were you. He'll be cross if you don't.'

'Oh, all right,' sighed Julia, opening the drawer where George kept his exercise book of business numbers with a sulky flounce. Emily and Julia's grandmother looked at each other, simultaneously raising their eyebrows.

Julia leant over to the black phone next to the sink. She dialled the number and asked for George. Then she turned around and gave the headpiece to her grandmother.

'You tell him,' she said. 'She's in St Vincents. I've got something to do.'

She ran up the stairs two and three at a time, so she didn't have to listen or be called on for further details. She could just imagine all the fuss and carry-on and Anabel lying there in the hospital bed lapping it all up and being terribly brave and George spending every possible spare minute visiting her and taking her flowers and making her special dishes so that she wouldn't have to eat all that dull hospital food . . .

Julia came to a halt in front of the television. Anabel, lying helpless in hospital, gratefully eating anything that was offered without thinking twice (not that she ever

73

seemed to think twice anyway). Anabel, passing away peacefully in the night, and the doctor coming and saying how sorry they were, these things happen, poor Anabel took a turn for the worse, they tried everything, nothing anyone could do, she was in such a weakened state as a result of her tragic accident. And the doctors wouldn't let anyone investigate because they'd be scared it was their fault and when everyone found out they'd lose all their customers.

The perfect murder. No exaggeration. Julia leant back against the television, thinking hard. The only thing was – where to get the poison? The same old problem. She couldn't go into a chemist like they did in books and ask for arsenic to kill the wasps that were infesting the summer house. She frowned. What had it said in the encyclopaedia? Something about common household substances. How dangerous they were, if people only knew. How poisonous.

That was the answer, surely, a common household substance. And it would have to be something that didn't taste too terrible because even Anabel wouldn't swallow a cake made of spray-on starch or mildew-remover.

Julia went into the kitchen, pulled out a stool and stood on it, peering into the food cupboards. Tins and bottles were so piled on top of each other that you never really knew what was there. In fact, you might rather not know, as they tended to be odd-sounding things (usually so old you couldn't read the price) that George picked up from time to time in dark forgotten corners of supermarkets and general stores. One of these things was sure to be poisonous, thought Julia, if you only had enough of it.

She read the labels. ARTICHOKE HEARTS. She couldn't make a cake out of artichoke hearts OLD-FASHIONED SEMOLINA SAUCE. That sounded too innocent. CAPERS IN CIDER VINEGAR. No, George was always eating capers and he wasn't dead yet.

Julia stood right up on her toes and reached the very back of the cupboard. Tins, more tins and dusty packets. Finally her hand fastened around the smooth cold neck of a tall bottle. She tugged it out, almost losing her footing, steadying herself by grabbing onto the swing door of the cupboard with her other hand.

Grasping the bottle carefully, Julia spat on the label and rubbed off a layer of red stickiness. She read it with disappointment. VANILLA ESSENCE. After all that it was only vanilla essence. She twisted open the lid and smelt it – strong, dark and very sweet. What a shame it wasn't poisonous.

But was it? Julia frowned again, remembering the paragraphs in the encyclopaedia. What had it said? About how something in small doses might not be poisonous, might even be essential to life, but when the dose was massively increased, it could bring about – what was it – 'a definite undesirable result'. Or desirable, actually, in this case.

She tasted a dab of the vanilla essence and wrinkled her nose. It certainly tasted poisonous. Could such a thing in small amounts be essential to life? It had to be: why else would it be called vanilla essence?

She closed the lid tightly and climbed down, returning the stool to its usual place. Already the cake she would make was forming itself in her mind – a big black delicious-looking chocolate cake, with an entire bottle of vanilla essence poured into it. That would finish Anabel off.

Julia took the bottle into her bedroom and hid it in the very back of the wide pull-out draw under her bed which was currently stuffed full of summer clothes. She couldn't make the cake right now – her grandmother might come at any moment and fix her with one of her awful suspicious stares and make her babble out an invention of guilty-sounding excuses. She would have to leave it until she was certain to have the kitchen all to herself.

11

George had, of course, immediately dashed out to see Anabel in hospital as soon as he had heard, abandoning his precious herrings without a thought. When he came home much later that evening he was full of how brave Anabel was, and how unlucky, and how sweet and sad she looked lying there in the bed in all that pain, surrounded by bits and pieces of equipment.

When Julia heard this, she seriously considered changing her murder plan – perhaps she could just sneak in in the middle of the night and pull out the wires that Anabel was attached to and her heart would stop beating. Julia had seen several people murdered this way on the television.

But when she went to the hospital the following day with George and her grandmother, she saw that Anabel was not attached to anything that important – all she had was a kind of pulley thing lifting her broken ankle up into the air and Julia couldn't see how yanking that off would affect her heart.

'Oh hello,' said Anabel in a weak voice, smiling pathetically.

George leant over and kissed her and gave her a

bunch of yellow flowers he'd bought from the florist six doors down from the delicatessen on the opposite side. Anabel blushed, but she didn't giggle. The accident must have injured her giggle nerve, Julia decided.

Julia's grandmother sat on a stool beside the bed and held Anabel's hand. Then from out of her handbag she produced a big box of liqueur chocolates, all wrapped up in different coloured metallic-looking paper. She put them on Anabel's bedside table.

'*Muchas gracias*,' said Anabel in one of the worst Spanish accents Julia had ever heard.

'Thank you for coming, Julia,' said Anabel.

'That's all right,' said Julia. 'I'll bring you my present next time.'

'Oh how sweet,' said Anabel.

Julia changed the subject. 'How many bones did you break?'

'Oh, I don't know,' whimpered Anabel, her smile fading, 'but I feel as if I'll never walk again.'

'Don't say that!' remonstrated George. 'We'll soon have you up and about. Running, jumping, dancing . . .'

'Oh please!' Anabel's face was pale with pain. 'I really can't think about it.'

George sank sorrowfully into apologies for his thoughtlessness. Julia looked about the room. There were five other people, all lying in the same sort of beds with various parts of their bodies done up in plaster and hanging in the air with bits of wire. They all had visitors except for one middle-aged man with a moustache and glasses, and he seemed a lot more relaxed than the ones with visitors. He was reading a copy of the *Reader's Digest* and chuckling to himself. He glanced up, caught Julia looking at him and smiled. Julia smiled back, then he went on reading. Both his legs were completely covered in plaster. Poor man, thought Julia. Perhaps he jumped into an empty swimming pool.

Some more visitors were coming into the ward. Julia recognised Anabel's parents, her brother and Patrice, who was dressed in leather and carrying a crash helmet. Julia noticed Mrs Sedlon's anxious face focusing immediately on Anabel, while Mr Sedlon, whose eyes were also fixed on Anabel, grabbed George's hand and said how do you do, nice to see you again.

'Hi!' said Julia, leaving Anabel's bedside and going over to Patrice, who was hanging back a little.

'Hi,' said Patrice.

'Can I have a go of your helmet?' asked Julia.

'Oh, all right,' said Patrice, handing it over. 'It's heavy, you know.'

It was very heavy and uncomfortable, and too big, of course. Julia couldn't imagine wearing such a thing for more than a few minutes – she felt as if her skull were caving in.

'Here.' Patrice pulled the wind visor down over Julia's eyes.

Julia looked around, but nobody was paying any attention to her – they were all looking at Anabel, who was offering them chocolates. Julia went over to the man reading the *Reader's Digest*. He winked at her and said, 'Are you from out of space?'

It was a weak joke, but Julia was grateful. With a short and painful struggle she pulled the helmet off and gave it back to Patrice. Then she went back to Anabel's bed and squeezed herself in next to George. Surely there must be a limit to the number of visitors one person could have?

'My poor darling,' said Mrs Sedlon. 'How long are they keeping you for?'

'I don't know,' said Anabel, with a woeful shake of her head. 'Maybe a week.'

'You'd better come home to Orange after that, love,' said Mr Sedlon. 'Get some real rest and recuperation.'

Julia's ears pricked up and George's face fell.

'Oh no, I'd never make the trip, really,' objected Anabel. 'Besides, I'd miss George.'

Mrs Sedlon looked down at Anabel sentimentally. 'Then I'll stay and look after you, darling,' she said. 'You can fit an extra body or two in the house, can't you?'

Patrice stared at Mrs Sedlon, distinctly alarmed.

'That would be okay, wouldn't it?' Anabel asked Patrice.

'Oh sure,' said Patrice, not attempting a smile, which was just as well, Julia thought, because it would have been a ghastly one.

'My poor darling,' said Mrs Sedlon again.

Julia removed herself from the loving circle. Little did they know, she thought. All this worry and concern for someone whose days were very definitely numbered. She pictured the bottle of vanilla essence in her mind's eye and sighed. Yes, murder was a nasty business.

'You look as if you're up to something.'

Julia jumped around. It was the man with the *Reader's Digest*. Surely he couldn't suspect? She frowned at him. He shrugged, smiling, his eyes falling back on the page in front of him.

She turned away. He couldn't suspect. No one could. It was ridiculous – a twelve-year-old girl murdering her father's girlfriend. Ridiculous! No one would think it for a moment. Still, Julia had always been fond of doing unusual things.

12

It was another two days before Julia was able to get time alone in the house to make Anabel's cake. She had only made a cake once before in her life, three years ago when she was in the Brownie Guides, and really the Brown Owl had made it and she'd just helped mix the stuff together.

She'd been too nervous to go searching through their recipe books in front of George or her grandmother, let alone make the cake. It wouldn't be nice for them to have to give evidence in court later on when the detectives tracked her down. When! Julia reprimanded herself. *If* they tracked her down, she meant of course. Still, there was something undeniably attractive about the image of herself standing in the dock accused of murdering Anabel, while George sat in the audience looking sorrowful and guilty. Mr and Mrs Sedlon would be there too, she supposed, but they wouldn't look guilty – they'd look terrible, like they wanted to kill her. Julia decided to stop thinking about the court case and start thinking about the cake.

She wanted a very simple recipe – just flour and sugar and whatever else you put in cakes – but the books didn't seem to have any of those. They all had strange ingredients she'd never heard of, like suet and Angostura Bitters, and she was sure there was none in the house. She knew better than anyone, having so recently inspected the cupboards.

Eventually she found a recipe for something called Devil's Food Cake and Angels' Food Cake that didn't look too difficult. She chose the Devil's because she didn't have to whip the butter until it was light and fluffy and because she preferred the name. Also, all the cocoa you had to put in would help disguise the taste of the vanilla essence.

Julia followed the instructions very conscientiously, as if it were a scientific experiment. She felt a bit like a mad scientist: one from the olden days who thought they could turn base metal into gold or make you live for ever or fall in love by drinking a special potion. Julia often thought she would have liked to be this sort of scientist if she'd lived a hundred years ago, but in this modern age what could she be? She had never seriously considered anything other than being a tightrope walker, and that was when she was four years old.

Once she had mixed everything together it looked quite appetising – dark brown and slushy. There were a few hard lumps of sugar and cocoa but she didn't worry about them – they would disappear when she cooked it, surely. Anyway, she didn't have time to be fussy. The cake had to be ready – cooking in the oven at least – by the time George and her grandmother got back from the hospital.

Julia looked at the brown mass and became very aware of the strength of her heart pulsing underneath her rib cage.

Taking a deep breath she went into her bedroom, pulled open the drawer under the bed and got out the fatal bottle. She went back into the kitchen, stood next to the bowl and untwisted the lid.

She wondered for a moment if she should say a magic word but decided that was too childish. Slowly she poured the essence into the swirled mixture. It floated on the top like oil on the ocean and smelt delicious. Julia took a wooden spoon and gradually folded it in until it had disappeared completely.

She pulled out from under the sink a round cake tin. It was a bit rusty but she covered the bottom and sides with grease-proof paper before pouring in the brown sloppy goo. It didn't seem to take up much room, but Julia optimistically decided that it would rise a lot when it was cooked.

The recipe said to bake in a moderate oven for forty-five minutes. Julia was not sure what a moderate oven was, but she twisted the temperature knob and lit the gas with a match the way George had taught her. Then she bent down and placed the cake tin on the middle rack. For some reason the thought of Hansel and Gretel pushing the wicked witch inside the oven popped into her head, and she stood up quickly and banged the door closed.

It was well over forty-five minutes by the time her grandmother and George got home and Julia had checked the cake's progress at least four times, but it still looked flat, wet and small, not at all like the cakes mothers made on television advertisements. It smelt nice though, which was the first thing George commented on when he came inside.

'That smells delicious!' He beamed and bent down to kiss Julia. 'Is it for me?'

'No, no,' Julia scolded. 'You can't eat things like that.'

'Oh yes, my diet,' said George, subdued. 'So you're going to eat it all yourself?'

'No,' said Julia carefully, trying to sound nonchalant. 'I made it for Anabel.'

'Oh you sweet child!' cried George, delighted. 'Anabel will love it! Do you hear that?' he said to Julia's grandmother, who was taking off her coat. 'Julia has made a cake for Anabel!'

'I heard,' said Julia's grandmother dryly, going into the kitchen and peering through the grease-encrusted window of the oven door. 'It's very small, isn't it?'

'I just did what the recipe said,' Julia defended herself. 'And anyway, it's only meant for one person.'

'I could have just a little slice,' George decided, bending at the knees to have a look himself.

'No you can't!' said Julia sharply. 'No one's allowed to eat any of it. Except Anabel. It's all for her.'

'Okay, okay.' George straightened up, grinning. 'Whatever you say.'

'How is Anabel, anyway?' asked Julia, trying to direct the conversation away from the cake.

'Ah, poor Anabel,' said George, getting himself a beer from the fridge. 'She's in a lot of pain.'

'I don't see why they can't give her something for the pain,' complained Julia's grandmother. 'In this day and age. What's modern medicine for?'

'Mama, they give her things, you know that,' said George. 'But there's a limit, no? They give her one tablet too many and –' (George made a squelching noise) 'no more Anabel.'

Julia's eyes widened. She couldn't help it. Incredible. Everything was playing into her hands. Now when Anabel didn't wake up one morning, no one'd think twice. They'd know it was the pain-killers. One too many. It was just extraordinary how things were working in her favour. Eloise would have to stop being an atheist if Julia told her about this.

'Shall I take the cake to Anabel, my love?' George broke in on her thoughts. 'I'm going tomorrow morning.'

'What about the shop?' Julia objected.

'It's okay. I spoke to Emily. She understands. It's an emergency. We're not too busy. Anyway, she loves Anabel.'

This series of feeble excuses did not impress Julia and she was sure they had not impressed Emily.

'You want to be careful,' she warned. 'Emily will leave you one of these days.'

'Doesn't Emily take all the time she needs when one of her grandchildren or nephews or cousins falls off a cliff or forgets to pull the parachute string?' said George, injured. 'We both agree – family comes first.'

But Anabel's not family, thought Julia fiercely, tears forming in her eyes. 'Oh sure, you take the cake!' she said roughly. 'I don't care. I'll ice it in the morning.'

And she left the room and went and lay on her bed face down for what seemed like hours, before she remembered to take off her clothes and sleep, having completely forgotten the wet, black cake baking slowly in the oven.

13

Julia had a bad dream that night. Everyone was in the dream – except George. Miss Marsden was there, her contact lenses staring right through Julia like x-ray eyes; Eloise, shocked, saying 'Why' and 'Why' again and again; her grandmother laughing cynically and shaking her head. There was Patrice, her long blue tongue flicking out and lashing her face like a whip while Anabel's brother rode round and around in circles on his motorbike. Mr and Mrs Sedlon sat by someone's grave – it must have been Anabel's – their soft affectionate eyes weeping blood which they wiped off with gumleaves, and the entire Salvation Army stood behind them, playing some happy loud hymn which nobody wanted to hear. But worst, sitting alone under a tree was Isabel, in a blue and white beach dress, with a huge pregnant stomach just like one of the photos in George's album, and Julia herself sat at her knees, sobbing and sobbing and shouting 'Stop it! Stop it! Stop it!'

It was the shouting that woke her. Her heart was beating loudly and her hands, which were damp with sweat, were grabbing onto the sheet. It was morning. She got out of bed at once and put on her school uniform. There were no clean socks in the drawer, so she found yesterday's under the wardrobe and put them on instead.

She went out to the kitchen, exhausted. Someone, probably her grandmother, had taken the cake out of the oven and placed it on the bench on a paper plate. There it sat, black and unappetising, and stinking of vanilla.

It was a very wet-looking cake, in spite of having been in the oven for who knows how long. Perhaps it didn't need icing after all. She could just dust it with icing sugar, like Brown Owl had done with the apple and bran loaf.

Suddenly she couldn't look at it any more. She couldn't even think about it. She found a big brown paper bag on top of the fridge and shoved the cake inside it. Then she took a black waterproof texta from the kitchen drawer and wrote on the bag:

Here is the cake for Anabel. I've gone to school.

She didn't feel like writing 'love' at the end. She didn't even feel like writing her name. She left the cake in its bag on the coffee table, picked up her satchel and ran out of the house.

'What's wrong with you?' asked Eloise during maths.

'Nothing,' replied Julia briefly, although she did feel rather ill: shaky at the knees and empty in the stomach.

'How's Anabel's leg?' said Eloise, not to be put off.

'Oh, I don't know.'

'My mother's sister broke her ankle once in America,' offered Eloise, adding, to compound the tragedy, 'on Christmas Day.'

Julia was not interested in Eloise's mother's sister. Her head was too full of wild, unpleasant thoughts of her own that she was desperate to banish but couldn't. She clicked the silver rings of her maths folder back and forth, pinching the skin of her forefinger so that the rings left little indentations as if very small teeth had bitten her.

Could Anabel already be dead?

She ran home quickly that afternoon. The sky was a pale purple-grey, and there was a faint thundering coming from the direction of the ocean. She wanted to know. She wanted it all to be over.

She walked through the door of the delicatessen with a cunningly innocent expression on her face. She even attempted a carefree whistle, but she was not the most powerful whistler at the best of times and she sounded like a waterlogged recorder.

She was actually surprised to see the shop still open. She would have thought George would put up black blinds and a little notice saying CLOSED UNTIL FURTHER NOTICE OWING TO FAMILY TRAGEDY. The people at the Greek delicatessen had done that once – then Julia found out later they'd only gone on holidays to the Gold Coast but they didn't want the robbers to think the place was empty.

Julia went behind the counter to where Emily was sitting with a cup of tea, reading a book. This was what she did when there were no customers and she'd run out of things to chop up. Emily read library books – six a week sometimes, George had told Julia in tones of awe. How can she keep track of all the different stories, George wondered.

'Hi Emily,' said Julia.

'Hello dear,' said Emily, taking a sip of tea and not looking up from her book.

Julia frowned. Hello dear? At a time like this? 'So, what's new?' she said. 'Anything exciting?'

'Oh no dear, very quiet today,' said Emily, licking one of her fingers and turning the page.

'Oh.' Julia was stumped. Perhaps Emily hadn't heard. 'George not back from the hospital yet?' she suggested.

'Oh yes, dear. He's been back a good while. He's taken the books upstairs. Catching up. It's all been at sixes and sevens, what with Anabel's accident.'

Had George forgotten to take the cake? What was going on? Was Anabel on a diet?

'He did visit Anabel today, didn't he?'

Emily sighed and looked up from her book. 'He's upstairs, Julia. If you really want to know, why don't you just pop up and ask him yourself.'

Julia took the hint. Her head in a jumble, she went up and found George sitting on the sofa with the account books spread out on the coffee table in front of him. George looked up and blew her a kiss.

'Hello my angel,' he said, shaking his head comically. 'Numbers, numbers, numbers.'

Julia sat down on the armchair opposite. 'Did you go and see Anabel today, Dad?'

'Oh yes, my love. Poor Anabel. So sweet. So brave.'

'Did you take her my cake?'

A peculiar expression came across George's face. He coughed and picked up a pen. 'Yes, yes. Of course.'

'Did she eat it?' said Julia.

George looked even more peculiar. 'Of course,' he snapped. 'Of course she ate it.'

'Well.' Julia paused, not sure what to say next. 'Did she like it?'

'Oh, she loved it,' said George at once with more conviction. 'It was delicious. Really delicious. She said,' he added quickly.

Julia was mystified. So far, all had gone according to plan, except that Anabel was apparently still alive. Could it be that it took quite a while to die of vanilla essence poisoning?

'Why don't you ring her and see how she is?'

George looked surprised, but relieved that the conversation had turned away from Devil's Food Cake. 'But why, my love? I'm going to see her tonight. After dinner. She's probably having a little sleep just now. But you can come with me tonight and ask her yourself.'

'Oh I can't,' said Julia, who had never seen a dead body and didn't particularly want to. 'I've got lots of homework.'

George shrugged. 'Poor Anabel. She would be so happy to see you. She loves you.'

Julia eyed George cynically, but poor George was obviously sincere. So innocent and sincere.

'Anabel's a teacher,' she pointed out. 'She'll agree I should do my homework before anything else.'

Julia spent the night watching television before getting into bed to read. She'd expected the phone to ring – George, the hospital, the police, Mr and Mrs Sedlon, Patrice, anyone – but nothing. It was maddening. And still George wasn't home. She lay in bed tugging at the buttons on her pyjama top. One was hanging on a single string, like a loose tooth. It only needed one yank – and . . .

She heard the door downstairs. Finally! George and her grandmother were home. She listened to them talking as they came up the stairs but she couldn't really make out any words. They seemed very calm. She considered switching off her bedside light and pretending to be asleep, but decided that would be too cowardly.

'Little by little,' she heard her grandmother say in Yiddish. George couldn't speak Yiddish, but he could understand it.

'What a thing to happen,' he said in Spanish.

Julia's eyes widened as if they were being propped open by toothpicks.

'You want something to drink, Mamita?' asked George.

But her grandmother said no, she was going straight to sleep, it was too late for her already and hospitals depressed her.

'Oh hospitals,' sighed George, opening the fridge door. 'Hospitals.'

George's voice sounded funny – not sad but very thoughtful, the way he sounded sometimes when he talked about Isabel. She heard him coming towards her room. He opened the door. 'Still up?' he said.

He came over to her, sat down on her bed and kissed her. 'My darling,' he said in English.

Julia licked her bottom lip. 'How's Anabel?'

'Ah, Anabel.' George stretched back his neck and smiled mysteriously. 'She's a little better you know. Better spirits. Not so much pain.'

Julia twisted the loose button on her pyjamas hard, but it didn't come off. 'Better?' she repeated.

'She's all right,' said George, tenderly. 'It's so sweet of you to worry about her. Sometimes she thought... well... it doesn't matter.'

'Did she say anything about the cake?' said Julia, feeling failure and despair loom over her like the dark cold shade of a skyscraper.

'Oh yes. The cake.' George stood up, and tousled Julia's hair. 'Of course, the cake. She said it was delicious. Thank you very much. Delicious.'

'She ate it all?'

'Oh yes,' said George, edging nervously out of the room. 'Oh yes. All of it. Delicious. Good night, my love. I don't feel one hundred per cent tonight. I'm going to sleep.'

He switched off her bedside light without asking her – something which she would normally have found infuriating, but now she scarcely noticed. She let her book about rutile mines in Africa fall to the floor.

Better? Better spirits? What was going on? Did Anabel flush her cake down the toilet out of politeness? Surely she wouldn't do that, not Anabel! Could vanilla essence be such a slow-acting poison? Or what was it she had read somewhere about people on their deathbeds – about how the patient seems suddenly to recover and then their head hits the pillow with a bang and that's the end. Could that be it? Perhaps they were already wheeling Anabel into the mortuary.

Julia rolled over and pressed her hip bones into the mattress. Tomorrow morning they would hear. Tomorrow the telephone would ring and wake them up as early as the doctor thought polite. And if it didn't? Julia refused to ponder this. Tomorrow they would hear.

14

But tomorrow there was no phone call and Julia went off to school as usual. George was still in bed when she left – he was feeling off-colour.

'Nothing serious,' her grandmother, who never stayed in bed, told her scornfully. 'He probably just ate something that disagreed with him.'

Julia felt at a loss as she walked to school. It was as if it had been going to be her birthday and she'd imagined all the excitement and the presents and the candles and the party, but when the day came, nothing happened. No one remembered or cared. She felt weak and empty.

She didn't want to go to school at all. She didn't want to sit in the classroom and talk to Eloise and draw a picture of a fish tank in her social studies book. Her pictures always seemed to end up ugly and grubby-looking and Eloise's so artistic. Not that Eloise ever said anything to rub it in. She just looked at Julia's picture and then at her own. That's all. Just like Miss Marsden did.

When she came to the corner to turn into the road that led to her school, Julia walked straight past it. She didn't plan to – her feet just kept on going. It was cold and the street was noisy and the footpath full of people with wet hair who had just got out of the shower and were hurrying to work in an office. Julia had never been inside an office, but Eloise had because her mother and father worked in one and sometimes they took her in on weekends. Eloise said that there were smelly leather chairs to swivel around on and cupboards full of paper and rubber bands and computers and photocopying machines.

Julia quickened her step – it was impossible to dawdle in such a busy atmosphere. She looked at her watch and saw that the morning bell would already have rung. She couldn't go now – she would get into trouble for being late and have to spend all lunchtime picking up papers and orange peel. But she couldn't go home either.

She would go to the hospital – that's what she would do. She would find out what was going on for herself. After all, maybe Anabel really had died last night and George was just keeping it from her because he thought she'd be upset. Or perhaps, if she wasn't dead, she was in intensive care having her stomach pumped and they were analysing her insides and saying, very strange, there seems to have been a noxious substance in the chocolate cake. Perhaps that was why George had been so funny when she asked him about the cake. Perhaps she was already the chief suspect and they'd put a policeman on her tail who was following her right at this moment!

Julia halted, and slid slyly behind a No Standing sign pole. She glanced swiftly about her. No sign of a policeman – but of course, he wouldn't be in uniform, but in disguise, to trick her.

She shook herself. She was being ridiculous again. No one could suspect her. Children don't commit murder – that is something confined to the adult world, like getting married and going to the office. Pull yourself together, she thought. That's what people said on TV. Pull yourself together. She would go to the hospital.

Julia, having walked to the hospital with George and her grandmother only a few nights before, could remember the way quite well, and she only took one wrong turn before she found herself in the park facing the hospital's back entrance. The same man who had been there last time was sitting surrounded by buckets of flowers and Julia said 'Hello' as she went past, but he didn't say 'Hello' back.

Inside, the hospital was quiet and tall, like a church, with peaceful white statues, flowers and a strong smell – not exactly the strong sweet smell of a church, of course – more like a floor that had just been scrubbed clean. She walked past the information desk and headed straight up the stairs. Anabel was on level two. It occurred to her as she climbed the stairs that if Anabel really had died already, she might run into her on the way up, all wrapped up in a white sheet being carried on a stretcher. She shuddered and increased her pace.

After two flights up, she turned to the right and hurried down the corridor, peeking into the various rooms on either side of her, which were full of people in beds looking up with sick, enquiring faces. Julia had a painful impulse to go and visit them all in turn. But then she noticed one of the faces was Anabel's.

Julia walked slowly into the ward, her eyes fixed on Anabel. She was not dead yet, nor did she look remotely near death. She was sitting up in bed drinking a cup of tea from an aqua hospital cup and reading a magazine. She gave Julia an uncomfortably welcoming smile.

'Oh Julia!' she said, with much more animation than she had shown the other day. 'How sweet!'

Julia approached Anabel's bed nervously. Out of the

corner of her eye she saw that the man with the moustache and the two broken legs was still there, reading the *Reader's Digest*, only perhaps it was a different issue by now.

'Sit down,' said Anabel, pointing to a rubber-topped stool. 'This is such a surprise. Shouldn't you be in school?'

Julia shrugged and sat down. She felt deeply gloomy – with a strange mixture of tremendous disappointment and tremendous relief.

'Actually, I was sort of wishing you might be able to come by,' said Anabel in a confidential tone. 'By yourself, I mean. Because there's something very particular I think we should talk about. Did George say anything last night?'

Julia frowned and shook her head.

'But do you think you might know what I'm talking about?'

Julia looked at the floor. So Anabel knew. She knew all about it. And what was worse, it sounded as though George knew as well. But how had they found out? How could they have guessed? Perhaps George had discovered the empty bottle of vanilla essence in the garbage bin. Julia wondered whether to prevaricate or just come clean. Anabel didn't seem to be very upset about it anyway. Perhaps people had tried to murder her before.

'You mean about the cake,' Julia said dully.

'Cake?' Anabel raised her eyebrows and knocked her glasses off her nose. 'What cake?'

'You know,' said Julia, impatiently. Why drag it out? 'The one I made for you.'

'Oh Julia, you made me a cake. How sweet,' said Anabel rather vaguely, adding quickly, 'But there's something else I must talk to you about.'

So she's forgotten already! thought Julia, astonished. Well, that's the last cake I make for you, ungrateful pig. Even if it was poisonous and meant to kill you, you might at least say something more than that.

'I must ask your opinion about something,' whispered Anabel, faintly blushing and taking a quick look around the room to see if any of the other patients were listening, which they all were, of course. 'George has asked me to marry him.'

Julia stared. Her eyes did not widen, her heart did not beat faster, her mouth did not drop open. She just stared.

'But naturally, I want to ask you what you think,' continued Anabel, a little louder and braver now the difficult words were spoken. 'I mean, of course, you're involved.'

Julia sat as still as a stone. She said, 'When did he ask you?'

'Yesterday,' said Anabel, with an almost-giggle. 'I was so shocked, I can tell you.'

'He asked you here?' said Julia, disbelieving. 'In the hospital? With all the people listening? And my grandmother?' She waved her arm around.

'It was late,' explained Anabel. 'I think they were all asleep. Even your grandmother was snoozing.'

I bet they weren't asleep, thought Julia. I bet they heard every word. Especially my grandmother.

'So,' said Anabel. 'I'm serious, Julia. What do you think? I mean, you're the first person I've told. I haven't mentioned it to Mum and Dad yet.'

'Why not?' said Julia, playing for time.

'Oh, they'd get too excited,' said Anabel. 'They've had their disappointments, you know. They had such high hopes of my brother and Patrice and nothing seems to be happening. They're just desperate for a wedding.'

Julia somehow found the strength to get up from the stool. She stood next to Anabel's bed and stared down at the pale orange blankets.

'Don't you like the idea?' said Anabel, in a small, sad little voice.

Julia looked up at Anabel. Yesterday. If her poison had worked, Anabel would have been dead yesterday. No time for proposals, high hopes, weddings, sad little voices, pathetic eyes, anything. Why hadn't it worked? What went wrong? Oh, if only it had. All she wanted was the three of them to be together for ever – her, George and Isabel's photograph.

'Don't you want us to get married?' said Anabel, smaller, sadder, trembling.

Oh shut up, thought Julia. I can't stand this. 'I don't care what you do!' she said crankily, struggling with herself. 'I mean, congratulations.'

Anabel's face broke into a huge smile, as if all her pain had disappeared in a miracle cure.

'Oh Julia!' she cried. 'How sweet!' She reached out as if she might like to kiss her. Julia took a few steps back.

'I've got to go now,' she said quickly. 'Back to school.'

'Oh course.' There were tiny tears in Anabel's eyes and she was wiping them out with a pink tissue. 'I'm so glad you came.'

'Well, goodbye then,' said Julia, turning around brusquely. She looked up and saw the man with the *Reader's Digest* looking speculatively at her.

'Hello,' she said, glad for an excuse not to have to say anything more to Anabel.

'Goodbye,' said the man more sensibly. He pointed up to the ceiling with his thumb. 'It's in the stars, my dear.'

Of course, he'd been listening to their entire conversation, thought Julia angrily as she took the lift back down to the ground floor. Nosy man, pretending to read his silly magazine. He must have read it twenty times by now.

But she remembered what he said. 'It's in the stars.' That meant it was fated. That what happens is meant to happen and you can't do anything about it. Her feeble attempt to change the course of all their lives with a bottle of vanilla essence was doomed from the start. Anabel was not meant to die just now, and it looked like Anabel and George were meant to get married and live happily ever after. And it was all her fault, anyway. She'd rung the number.

The lift opened, and she thought of Eloise who was an atheist and didn't believe in the stars. Eloise didn't believe in anything. Julia wished she could be like that, but it seemed as though her life were determined not to let her.

15

Julia went straight back to school. She no longer cared what punishment she might receive and she wandered blatantly into the empty school yard without a trace of self-consciousness. She told Miss Marsden she'd been to visit her father's fiancée in hospital, and Miss Marsden seemed to think that that was a perfectly reasonable way to spend the morning and told her to sit down quickly and get out her spelling book.

At recess, Julia told Eloise:

'They're getting married.'

Eloise squealed. 'Really and truly! I thought you just said she was George's fiancée to make it sound better.'

'No, they're really getting married,' Julia said.

'So? When?' Eloise loved weddings. She had already been a flower-girl three times.

'I don't know when,' said Julia, surprised, as she had not particularly considered this. 'I suppose as soon as her leg gets better and she can walk without crutches, maybe.'

'Oh, but some people get married at hospital beds,' began Eloise who knew all about such things, but seeing Julia's face she continued quickly, 'oh but other people go on being engaged for years and years and then they break it off.'

Julia could not see George waiting for years and years. He was simply not that kind of person. She could not take any false comfort there.

'Is she going to move in with you, or you with her?' asked Eloise, in a more practical vein.

Julia looked shocked. Here was another thing that had not even entered her head. She hoped very much that Anabel would move in with them. Even if Anabel's house was in a quiet street with a big garden and an ancient fish pond, Julia did not want to leave the shop, and she certainly did not want to live with Patrice.

'She told me,' Julia announced baldly to George when she walked into the delicatessen that afternoon. Neither Emily nor her grandmother were there – only two customers arguing over which kind of pressed chicken to buy.

George's face fell, and a look of panic entered his eyes.

'She told you!' he said, alarmed. 'But how did she know?'

Julia rolled her eyes. 'What do you mean, how did she know? You told her, didn't you?'

'I did?' said George, looking astonished.

Julia folded her arms and turned away in disgust. Well, if he were going to try and deny it . . .

'Julia, my love.' George's voice was full of sorrow, and he held her by the shoulders. 'I couldn't help it. I just couldn't resist.'

'Oh yeah.' Julia was unimpressed.

'I know, I know, it's bad for me!' George half-wailed. 'But such a smell! What could I do? You shouldn't have trusted me with it!'

The couple arguing about the pressed chicken finally came to a not very amicable agreement, and George picked up their choice and started cutting it into thin slices on the machine, a woebegone expression on his face.

'What are you talking about?' said Julia, a sick alarm creeping into her stomach.

'What am I talking about?' said George, casting his eyes briefly up at the ceiling in a gesture of grief and shame. 'The cake! The cake! Your beautiful cake! That you made for Anabel!'

Julia swallowed. 'You ate the cake I made for Anabel?'

'I know. I'm a dog. Horrible. Evil. Hit me. I ate the cake!' said George dolefully in English to the pressed chicken couple.

'How do you feel?' said Julia urgently. 'Do you feel all right?'

'Guilty!' cried George. 'Awful! How could I!'

'I mean, how do you feel in your body,' said Julia. 'Do you feel sick?'

'Oh, I'm all right now,' replied George, calmer. 'But it was very rich, my love. This morning I could hardly get up. So queasy. But what a flavour! What a taste!' He smacked his lips. 'What did you put in it?'

He wrapped up the chicken in rough white paper and plastic and handed it to the couple, taking their money and giving them their change.

Julia gazed at George in horror. George ate the cake! George! She poisoned her own father! For a moment she thought she would faint.

'I'm so sorry, my darling,' said George, his head hanging, full of remorse. 'Can you forgive me?'

Julia suddenly threw herself at him and wrapped her arms around his stomach. Oh George! Her own George! She was only lucky that he was so big and strong – his

102

powerful constitution must have saved him! She could have killed him! Her father! All because of that silly Anabel.

Julia lifted her head from George's stomach and looked him straight in his kind green eyes. 'You asked Anabel to marry you!' she said sternly. 'I know you did. She told me.'

George coughed slightly. He scratched his calf with his foot. He gave Julia a slight, apologetic smile. 'Oh well,' he said, 'seeing she told you.'

'Yes,' said Julia, unwavering. 'I visited her this morning and she told me.'

'Well, yes,' agreed George uneasily. 'Well, I asked her and she didn't ... um ... say no. If you know what I mean ...'

At that moment Emily walked in, carrying a shopping bag of fruit and vegetables.

Julia said to her in English, 'George and Anabel are getting married.'

'Really?' said Emily, unperturbed, putting her shopping bag down behind the counter. Emily's nephews and nieces were always getting married. 'Well, that's nice. Congratulations, George.'

'Thank you,' said George, looking furtively at Julia.

'That's a turn up for the books,' Emily remarked.

'Er, yes,' said George.

'I'm sure Julia's pleased, aren't you dear?' said Emily in warning tones.

'Well, I wouldn't marry her,' said Julia bluntly. 'Not if you paid me.'

'Of course you wouldn't!' beamed George, laughing and kissing her on both cheeks. 'But I would, if you took money from me!'

'Have you told your mother?' enquired Emily.

'Er, not yet.' George became nervous again.

'I should,' said Emily. 'She'll be delighted.'

'You think so?' said George hopefully.

'Oh yes,' said Emily. 'She's been waiting for the day.'

'How do you know?' Julia objected. 'You don't even speak the same language.'

Emily sniffed. 'There are things beyond mere language, Julia,' she said, turning on the sink tap and washing her hands. 'We understand each other all right, on that subject, anyway.'

'Ah yes! The music of the heart!' cried George enthusiastically, 'The . . .'

Emily turned off the tap and wiped her hands on her apron. 'Well, something like that.' She looked at George indulgently.

Oh the music of the heart, thought Julia grimly. Well, that's something I wouldn't know about. And wouldn't want to. Anyway, what would Anabel know of the music of the heart? She sighed. More than she did, it seemed.

16

On Saturday afternoon, one and a half weeks later, Anabel came out of hospital. George, Julia and Julia's grandmother all went to Anabel's place to welcome her home.

They arrived at the Newtown street before Anabel did and no one else was home. George switched on the car radio, but all he could find was football and a passionate discussion in a language unknown to them, so he switched it off. He turned round and tweaked Julia's chin – she was sitting in the back. She scowled and looked out the window up and down the street. A couple of boys were playing king pin on the footpath opposite and a man was delivering a case of soft drink to the corner shop. It was hot and sunny.

Julia's grandmother leant back in her seat and closed her eyes. Julia took off her green knitted cardigan and began to sing a song they'd learned at school for education week:

I'm bewitched by a girl named Sofia
With a nose like a full-grown balloon

What can I do? What can I do?
Enchanting Sofia I'm mad about you!

Neither George nor her grandmother knew the words, so Julia had to sing it by herself, and she got louder and quicker with every repeated verse until finally George turned around with an apologetic smile (he had been particularly gentle with her lately):

'Please, my love. My head.'

Julia subsided and sulked. George couldn't stand it when she sulked. But just then Mrs Sedlon came driving around the corner with Mr Sedlon in the front seat next to her and Anabel and her plaster cast and crutches in the back. Behind them, looking like a police escort of a visiting dignitary, came Patrice and Anabel's brother, each on their own motorbike. The street's near silence was overcome by noise and exhaust.

George leapt out of his seat and bounded over to where Mrs Sedlon was parking. He extracted Anabel from the back seat like a surgeon with a difficult appendix. Anabel was wearing a red and white dress Julia had never seen before. She wondered if George had bought it for her.

'Take the crutches!' George shouted at Julia, conveniently forgetting that she was sulking.

Julia forgot as well and ran over and picked them up. She pushed the pads under her arms and tried to hop along like you were supposed to, but she wasn't strong enough.

'Takes a bit of practice, dear,' said Mrs Sedlon cheerfully.

Julia quickly pretended that she hadn't been trying, slipped from the crutches under her arms and carried them normally. 'Hello,' she said. 'How are you?'

'What a relief,' said Mr Sedlon, sweating a little as he

emerged from the boot with Anabel's bag. 'So good to have poor little Anabel home again.'

Julia did not reply but hurried inside the cool dark house and into the living room. Patrice was already sitting down, taking a gold cigarette lighter out of the pocket of her leather jacket and lighting up. She smiled briefly at Julia.

'So your father's getting married again,' she said between puffs. 'What do you think about it?'

Julia shrugged. Patrice muttered something to Anabel's brother who had just come into the room.

'George is helping Anabel put her things in the back room,' Patrice explained to Julia, although she had not asked. 'We've rearranged things so she doesn't have to go up and down stairs all day.'

'That's good,' said Julia, unconvincingly.

Mr Sedlon marched into the living room, clapping his hands together. 'Come now, let's toast the happy couple, shall we?'

'Where are they?' enquired Mrs Sedlon, peering round from Mr Sedlon's large shoulders.

'In the back room,' said Patrice, stubbing out her cigarette in an ashtray already full of butts.

I bet they're kissing, thought Julia. 'I'll go and get them,' she volunteered.

But Mr Sedlon had already poked his head into the corridor, and was now shouting, 'Anabel! George! Come on!'

Anabel's returning giggle echoed around the dark house. Julia ran out into the corridor and saw that George was carrying Anabel and her plaster cast all the way up. He staggered into the living room and laid Anabel very gently and carefully into an armchair, then stood back, gazing fondly at her. So did everyone else, except for

Patrice and Julia, and Anabel's brother had disappeared out into the kitchen to clink glasses, as usual.

'Right,' said Mr Sedlon. 'All present and correct. A toast to welcome Anabel home and to congratulate the happy couple.'

He went out to the kitchen and returned after a short discussion with Anabel's brother with a tray of champagne glasses and a tall elegant bottle of pink liquid.

'Bubbling grape juice,' said Mr Sedlon generally, answering the unspoken question.

Anabel's brother came out with more glasses and Mr Sedlon opened the bottle. It even pops like champagne, thought Julia, surprised. Julia's grandmother, who was feeling the heat, sat down with a grunt on the sofa, but everyone else stood up, as if they were in the presence of royalty.

Mr Sedlon filled up the eight glasses – or half-filled them, as there was not enough in the bottle to be really generous. He raised his glass.

'God bless you both!' he said. 'Congratulations!'

'*Mazal tov*,' said Julia's grandmother from underneath them, with surprising vigour.

'Was that Russian?' asked Mrs Sedlon politely. 'Your ancestors were Russian, I believe,' she said to George. 'Anabel was telling us something of that kind.'

'I am a descendant of Abraham!' said George grandly.

'That was Yiddish,' said Julia. 'And she's from Romania, not Russia.'

'Oh yes,' said Mrs Sedlon, to whom Russia and Romania amounted to much the same thing. She turned to George and Anabel again and said, 'Well. Tell us! Have you set a date?'

Anabel blushed and looked at George and George blushed and looked at Anabel. 'Oh well,' said George.

'We thought in a year,' said Anabel. 'This time next year.'

'That's nice,' said Patrice dutifully, downing her glass of sparkling grape juice with a grimace.

'I hope your leg's better by then,' contributed Anabel's brother, making Julia jump in shock as she had never heard him speak before.

'Anabel will be hurdling by then!' declared George, proud of the new word he had learned from an Olympic broadcast on television.

'Well, not hurdling, I hope,' said Mrs Sedlon primly.

'Anabel was never much of a one for track and field,' chortled Mr Sedlon. 'But you look like you could run fast,' he said to Julia with a jovial poke in the ribs. 'You're skinny enough!'

Julia didn't answer. She was afraid she might cry. She didn't feel well and she didn't feel happy and she didn't like the sticky taste of the sparkling grape juice or the smell of the cold living room and she didn't like Patrice's leather jacket or her cigarette lighter.

George pulled her thin shoulders over to him and kissed the top of her head.

'Julia can be the bridesmaid,' said Mrs Sedlon. 'You'll like that, won't you dear?'

'No,' said Julia.

'Come here,' said Julia's grandmother to her in Spanish, patting the empty place beside her on the sofa. 'Come here with me.'

Julia went and squeezed herself next to the fat soft warmth of her grandmother's hip.

'You funny child,' Julia's grandmother murmured in Spanish, softly, so that George couldn't hear. 'What do you think the world is for?'

Julia didn't answer. Truthfully she had no idea what

109

the world was for, but she hadn't expected it was for George to marry Anabel in.

'You think the three of us would live like this for ever?' said Julia's grandmother. 'A man with his mother and daughter until his funeral?'

'It wasn't always just you and me,' said Julia in a small voice.

Julia's grandmother closed her eyes for a moment. She had large pale-veined eyelids and her long eyelashes rested on her cheeks. 'Ah, Isabel,' she sighed. 'Poor beautiful Isabel. You're right. Isabel for him was everything.' She opened her eyes and looked gently at Julia, twisting her hair around her fingers. 'But Isabel is a memory, Julia. A memory and a photograph. A man can't live with only a photograph.'

'Well, here's to them!' said Patrice loudly, raising her empty glass. 'And welcome home Anabel.'

'To them!' echoed Mr and Mrs Sedlon, and possibly Anabel's brother. 'Congratulations!'

George caught Julia's eye and smiled with such tenderness that it touched her heart and she had to smile back despite herself. Would he have smiled at her like that if Anabel had died? Especially if he had known that she had poisoned her?

She suddenly realised that George could not have found the empty bottle of vanilla essence in the garbage bin anyway, because she had forgotten to throw it away. It must still be standing there in the kitchen cupboard. All that evidence, staring them in the face.

Julia groaned inwardly. What a hopeless murderer she was! First, the wrong person got the poison; secondly, the poison hadn't proved very effective anyway; and thirdly, she couldn't even hide the clues.

She looked at George, holding Anabel's hand adoringly. Oh well, under the circumstances it was probably just as well. Her grandmother had a point. You can't hold the hand of a person in a photograph.

'A year's a long way off,' said Eloise reasonably when Julia told her before school assembly on Monday.

'I suppose so,' said Julia. 'There's nothing I can do about it, anyway.'

'Oh don't say that!' Eloise objected. 'There's lots of things you can do.' She giggled. 'You could murder her, for instance.'

Julia looked hard at Eloise, with an expression of deepest scorn and sorrow. 'Oh honestly, Eloise,' she said. 'Don't be so childish. You don't just murder people you don't like.'

'Well, what do you do with them then?' Eloise retorted.

Julia heaved a worldly sigh. It was not often that she felt more grown up than Eloise. 'You learn to live with them,' she said at last. 'That's all.'

Was that all? Well she could try, anyway.